THE ARPINO ASSIGNMENT

THE ARPINO ASSIGNMENT

GEOFFREY TREASE

Illustrated by
PAUL LEITH

WALKER BOOKS
LONDON

First published 1988 by Walker Books Ltd
184-192 Drummond Street, London NW1 3HP

First printed 1988
Printed in Great Britain by
Billings and Sons Ltd, Worcester
Typeset by Graphicraft Typesetters Ltd, Hong Kong

British Library Cataloguing in Publication Data
Trease, Geoffrey
The Arpino assignment.
I. Title
823'.914 [J]   PZ7
ISBN 0-7445-0810-X

"To set Europe ablaze..."

Winston Churchill's directive to the SOE
(Special Operations Executive)
established in July 1940 after Hitler's triumph in the West.

ONE

"YOU! I want yewww!"

Sergeant-major Trappe had a voice of whiplash quality.

The three young defaulters, peeling potatoes outside the cook house, rose as one man. After months of infantry training in all weathers, they were incapable of turning pale.

"Only you, Weston! The Professor," Trappe added with scornful impatience.

Rick braced himself for another unpleasant encounter. The sergeant-major hated him. Not because he was a bad soldier – Rick might hate the stupid monotony of these early months in the army, but he knew that they were just something you had to endure.

Trappe was always trying to catch him out, but with no success until yesterday, and then only for a faint smear on his polished cap badge. Gleefully he had added Rick to the defaulters condemned to a session of spud bashing.

Normally Trappe could find no fault with Rick's turn-out or the way he was learning the basic skills of soldiering. Early on, though, Rick had made the fatal mistake of asking intelligent questions. Even worse, when the squad themselves were questioned after a demonstration of the bren-gun or the throwing of hand-grenades, Rick had answered in his own words instead of parroting the phrases of the manual.

Trappe disliked men who thought for themselves. It was not what the army was about. Private Weston also read books. Trappe had spotted them at kit inspection. Private Weston had probably passed exams. Trappe distrusted education and had carefully avoided it from his childhood.

"Yes, you, Professor! You're wanted. Company Office."

"What about these potatoes, sir?"

Trappe swore at the innocent vegetables. Let the other lads finish them. "Come on! Can't keep the major waiting."

Rick stared. He seldom had any contact with officers. Recruits lived a lowlier existence, harassed by corporals and sergeants or, at the highest and most horrible level, by Sergeant-major Trappe.

He had no choice but to fall into step beside his persecutor as they crossed the barrack square.

Trappe asked, out of the corner of his mouth, "What's all this about, then?"

Rick realized with some pleasure that Trappe himself

did not know. And Trappe hated not knowing.

"I've no idea, sir."

"Sure?" Trappe sounded deeply suspicious.

"Yes, sir."

"Could be bad news from home." This thought seemed to cheer the sergeant-major considerably.

Rick felt a sudden chill. Suppose Trappe's guess was right? So far as he knew, all was well at home. Though his father had been a bit of a crock since 1940 – he'd been wounded at the Dunkirk evacuation – his general health was sound. Young Sally was always fit as a ferret. But accidents could happen.

"If it's a funeral," Trappe promised, "you'll get compassionate leave. But it's gotta be a real close relative." Too bad, he implied, if it isn't a near-and-dear.

They reached Company Office. Trappe knocked on the inner door, flung it open and barked – but somehow barked respectfully – "Here he is, sir. Private Weston, R., sir!"

"Bring him in, sergeant-major."

"Sir!" Trappe swung round. "Quick – march! Left, right, left, right… *halt!*" Rick finished smartly in front of the desk, stamping his feet and saluting.

The major looked up cheerfully, not like one about to console the bereaved. "Weston? Richard Weston?"

"Sir!"

"Stand at ease. Stand easy. You can sit down."

"Thank you, sir."

"Cap – *off!*" snarled Trappe, scandalized by this humane treatment.

"Thank you, sergeant-major." The company commander unlocked a drawer and took out an envelope. Its red seal was broken. Rick read the words, upside down, TOP SECRET. The major glanced up at Trappe, who was hovering like a frustrated vulture. "He'll need a railway warrant. London. And a forty-eight hour pass. Make them out, will you? That'll be all, I think."

"Sir!" Trappe could not very well slam the door behind him, but his exit was impressive. When the vibrations had died away the major smiled at Rick. He had an inquisitive expression.

"Someone at the War Office seems to want you. Rather urgently."

Rick's jaw dropped. "May I ask why, sir?" It was the kind of question that made him unpopular with Trappe.

The major merely said, "I was hoping *you* could tell *me*." He took a smaller envelope from the larger one. "Take this. Don't open it. Hand it in at reception. They'll tell you where to go. One thing: not a word to anyone. None of your mates here. Or girlfriends if any. Understand?"

"Yes, sir."

The major glanced at his watch. "Right. There's a London train in fifty minutes. You can just make it. Pick up your railway warrant as you go out. Double off to your hut, now – change into best battledress. We'll have a truck waiting at the guard room to run you to the station. And – Weston..."

"Sir?"

"This may be a flap all about nothing. But, in case you don't come back to us – best of luck."

"Thank you, sir." In a daze Rick stood up, remembering in the nick of time to put on his cap before he saluted. But for the anguished yelp of the sergeant-major he would have passed through the outer office without collecting his vital travel documents.

TWO

It was good to be in London again, even the London of 1943, shabby after four years of war. Hitler's bombs had torn gaps in the streets, there were empty shop windows, sandbagged doorways, posters crying DIG FOR VICTORY and CARELESS TALK COSTS LIVES; but there was a jauntiness in the air. Complete strangers joked together in comradeship. People hurried along with an air of purpose.

Everywhere a babel of foreign voices... Dutch, Belgian, Polish, Norwegian, Free French – and of course everywhere, the Yanks. Other troops from different parts of the Empire: a black man in RAF blue with *Jamaica* on his shoulder or a turbanned Sikh from India.

It was late afternoon when Rick reported at the War Office. He was told to sit down and wait. After some minutes a man behind the porter's window called, "You're to see Colonel Davis. Just round the corner. You'll need a pass." He scribbled. Picking up the slip of paper, Rick saw that he was to go to a hotel.

That sounded cheerful. But it proved to be the drabbest corner of London he had seen that day. The glass canopy over the entrance had been shattered, its ornamental ironwork twisted and discoloured by fire. The swing doors had gone. There was a narrow entry protected by a blank wall of concrete blocks. Clearly the place had been requisitioned by the government.

The doorman took his pass. "You're expected. They rang through. Fourth floor." Another man limped into view, waved Rick into an ancient lift and clanged the gates. They soared, whining, into the upper gloom. Then they went along a corridor of flaking gilt and fly-spotted mirrors. The man paused at a door, tapped. A deep voice called, "Come in!" and Rick entered.

Colonel Davis was white-haired and burly, surprisingly not in uniform but in lumpy tweeds and darned cardigan. He reminded Rick of his own grandfather, just come in from gardening. Surprisingly, too, when he told Rick to sit down, he spoke in fluent Italian.

Instinctively Rick answered in the same language. He had scarcely spoken it since the war began, almost four years ago now, in 1939. Yet the vibrant syllables, familiar from babyhood, took him instantly back to the sunshine and the cypresses, which was odd, for in fact they were sitting in what had once been a hotel bathroom, all tiled walls and frosted glass. The colonel sat behind a trestle table. Another table-top was laid over the bath, draped with a brown army blanket which left only the old-fashioned claw feet and two brass taps in view.

"Fine!" The colonel switched to English. "Your accent sounds all right. But of course – isn't your mother Italian?"

"*Was*, sir. She died just before the war."

"I'm sorry, Weston."

"Thank you, sir." Rick swallowed. "But I've often thought this war would have broken her heart. England having to fight against Italy." He remembered this was an interview. He mustn't let his voice tremble, mustn't let emotion show. "I was brought up bilingual from the start," he said. "Both my parents were very keen on that."

"And there were the holidays at Castel Sant' Arpino."

Rick stared. "You know about Sant'Arpino?"

"Of course. But – just now – *I* am asking the questions."

"Sorry, sir. But I've never met anyone before who's even heard of the place."

"That's been our problem. Not a tourist place. We tracked down your father because of some learned article he'd written about digging up the old Roman villa there. How often did you go with him?"

"Every summer, sir, up to 1939. And two Easter holidays."

"Did you find the excavations interesting?"

Rick made a face. "It was a bit slow. Pecking away so patiently, never finding anything sensational..."

"What else did you do with yourself?"

"Oh, just mucked about, sir. Kicked a ball around with the local boys. My mother said it was bad for my Italian. You know how every region speaks its own

13

brand. It marks you out rather."

"What else did you do?"

"Oh, long walks in the hills. And I hired a bike. Rusty old ruin – but I got about. Awful roads."

"But you got about?" The colonel sounded pleased. "Must have explored every by-road, pretty well."

"Excellent." The colonel pondered. "Weston, you might be rather useful to us."

"Useful, sir?"

"Perhaps. You realize that this conversation must remain absolutely secret? Not a word even to your father. Should he ask."

"Of course, sir." But Rick was utterly mystified.

"I was speaking to him – briefly – only yesterday. It's urgent to find someone who knows that Sant'Arpino area. But I hadn't realized your father was now disabled."

"He was wounded during the evacuation at Dunkirk..."

"So for him a parachute jump simply isn't on."

"A parachute jump?" Rick tried to picture his father in parachute harness instead of the black gown of an Oxford lecturer in Ancient History.

"So that leaves you. But it's a volunteer job. You must make up your own mind."

Rick's lips were dry. "A parachute jump?" he repeated.

"You'd be given some training. But you'd have to learn fast. What you might call a crash course." The colonel chuckled. Rick did not entirely appreciate the grim joke. "Now," the colonel went on, "if you have any questions, it's your turn."

"What do you want me to *do*, apart from the parachute jump?"

14

"That will depend on circumstances – when you get to Sant'Arpino. Have you heard of the SOE?"

"No, sir."

"Good! We don't *want* people to know about it – unless they're in it. SOE stands for Special Operations Executive. A very undercover outfit indeed. Churchill set it up himself in 1940 when the Nazis had overrun so many countries. The object, in Churchill's own words, 'to set Europe ablaze'."

"But – Sant'Arpino..." began Rick doubtfully.

"I know, I know. A sleepy little town. But we hear of some underground resistance stirring in the hills there. And helping the Resistance is the main job of the SOE. Wherever the conquered countries have formed an underground movement against the enemy."

"You mean for sabotage, sir? That sort of thing?"

"Yes – anything that hits the enemy where they're not expecting it. Sabotage, armed resistance, whatever's possible. We can't lay down rules from here. The man on the spot has to improvise, act on his own initiative. Up to now, the Italians haven't shown much sign of developing a resistance movement. Of course, their government is on Hitler's side, but there *are* anti-Fascists —"

"Oh, there are, sir. I remember —"

"Yes, what do you remember?"

"Slogans on walls, sir. Rude drawings of Mussolini. And the older people always muttering about the good old days before he seized power. And now we've kicked his armies out of North Africa I expect even his own supporters must be wavering."

"Well, there's certainly something moving in the Sant'Arpino area. It's vital that we make contact quickly and find out just what – and how the SOE can help stir things up a bit more. We need someone who knows that country, who can talk to the people. You made friends, I imagine?"

"I'd say so. The boys I played with may be away in the army now, but there were shopkeepers and old Lamberti who kept the hotel where we stayed..."

"Could you trust them?"

Rick thought quickly. "Not all. There's a war on. If I walked in today, I can't be sure how they'd all react."

"Would you take a chance?" The colonel's shrewd eyes appraised him. "We have one experienced major with fluent Italian, but he doesn't know that district and of course he can't speak like a local. That's where *you*'d come in. Major Blair would be in charge, of course, but your special knowledge and contacts would be invaluable. It's dangerous. You can have time to think – but not long."

Rick had already decided. An escape from drill and drudgery! Above all, an escape from the sergeant-major. "I'd like to have a go, sir."

"That's the spirit. You'll be given an immediate commission." The colonel smiled at Rick's astounded expression. "The Italians won't take much notice of you as Private Weston. You look too young for a captain. Lieutenant, I think."

With Colonel Davis practical difficulties melted like ice on a hot stove. Of course Rick's unit would release him. "We have power to take any volunteer we want from any of the three services. No, you needn't even report back – your personal kit will be forwarded. It'll be better if no one at your old unit sees you again."

Rick had one regret about this. It would have been wonderful to walk through the camp gates just once more – in lieutenant's uniform – and see old Trappe

16

goggling at the badge of rank on his shoulder, apoplectic at having to salute him.

But the colonel told him not to waste time and money at the tailor's. "We're not going to drop you in uniform. That would be wasting you as well."

Rick's spine crept. If not in uniform — which he obviously couldn't be — he was liable to be shot as a spy. But it was too late to back out now.

The colonel was scribbling a number on a scrap of paper. "Report at ten o'clock tomorrow morning. No, not here. This number — in Baker Street. The SOE doesn't put up brass plates to advertise itself, but it works from Baker Street and various buildings in the side-streets round there. This is the one you go to. The department that will handle the Arpino Assignment. That's the code name for this operation. You'll be given a code name yourself." The colonel shook hands and wished him luck.

I'll need it, thought Rick, still a little dazed as he strode away down Whitehall. He bought an evening paper and glanced at the headlines. The Prime Minister had been in North Africa, visiting the victorious generals. Where in the Mediterranean, in this hopeful summer of 1943, would the Allies strike next?

Would it be Italy?

THREE

"On our way – at last." Blair's soft, faintly Scottish voice was just audible against the roar of the climbing Halifax.

The major's usual calm could not entirely conceal his tension.

So too, when Rick had first met him ten days ago, Blair's cordial greeting had not been able to disguise his disappointment, alarm almost, at the youth of the assistant assigned to him. "Code name 'Newboy'?" he'd queried gruffly. "I'm 'Tartan'. Equally appropriate." His grey-blue eyes had been cool and sceptical. "Fluent Italian, I'm told. Local knowledge. Very useful. See why they chose you." And Rick had thought to himself, heart in boots but beginning to stir indignantly: he thinks I'll be no good. I got on this by accident, Italian mother, holidays at Sant'Arpino – no other qualifications whatever. He's summed me up, fresh from school, no experience, dead loss. I'll just have to show him, that's all...

Now, huddled there in the darkness aft of the bomb bay, he answered respectfully, "Yes, sir. I thought we never *would* get started."

"In this game you've got to plan to the last detail."

Rick knew. One slip, and you could be looking down the gun barrels of a firing squad. But the SOE, the Special Operations Executive, with its back-room experts scattered in anonymous offices round Baker Street, must be the most thorough outfit in the world.

Outfit was the right word. Every stitch of the shabby clothing he was now wearing was of Italian make. Every shred could have passed the tests of a Scotland Yard murder inquiry. The SOE spared no effort to find the proper clothes for every agent dropped into enemy territory. If necessary it would obtain the fabrics and enlist the tailors – refugee anti-Nazi Germans and Austrians, or Frenchmen or Poles – to make them up in the appropriate foreign styles.

In only two details did Rick's disguise vary from what any young Italian might have worn: his left boot concealed in its lining a thin flexible saw with tiny teeth of formidable cutting power. "Normally it's for brain surgery," Blair had explained. "But mighty handy for getting out of tight places."

"Special operations indeed, sir!"

The other variation was an ordinary-looking button which contained a miniature compass, an RAF device for finding one's way after a crash in unknown country. The RAF uniform button had a crested top which unscrewed to disclose the compass inside. Disguised agents wore a plainer type as a trouser fly button.

Tonight, before take-off, their conducting officer had made a final check in the briefing room of the Derna airfield. They had all stripped to the skin – Blair, Rick and the RAF sergeant, Charlie Morgan, who completed the team as its wireless operator, or "pianist" in service slang.

Pockets were turned out. Not the smallest clue must be left to show that they had only recently arrived from England. Blair groaned when his favourite cigarettes were confiscated. He could take only an Italian brand.

That did not trouble the others. Rick had never become a serious smoker. Charlie had the Welshman's two great enthusiasms, for singing and for Rugby football. Tobacco, he had found, did not improve his performance at either.

Maps, even Italian maps, would look suspicious. So they, like the pistols, must be carried for the present in the case containing Charlie's two-way radio. This was a shabby, everyday-looking suitcase which would not normally attract notice, but if ever it were searched it would instantly give them away, so that the addition of maps and pistols could hardly make matters any worse. At the very first opportunity that give-away suitcase must be stowed safely out of sight.

"If you get lost," said the conducting officer genially, "you've always got your hankies." Blair snorted in disgust.

They had been issued with rather special handkerchiefs Italian-made but treated by a Lancashire firm co-operating with the SOE. Maps had been printed on them in invisible ink. They could be read only when soaked with a suitable liquid. Ordinary water or sweat must not reveal them by accident and unexplained bottles of other fluid would invite questions. "Luckily," Blair had already explained to Rick, "there happens to be one suitable liquid we're never without. But as an aid to map-reading we don't use it unless we have to."

Then, an hour or two ago, they had boarded the plane under a brilliant moon, newly risen. It made one feel rather exposed, thought Rick. But the RAF insisted on good visibility when landing parachutists if it were a blind drop with no "reception committee" to mark out the zone with lights.

By now they must be well out over the Med.

For jumps such as theirs a hole had been cut out of the floor of the Halifax and covered with a hatch until the pilot flashed his red warning light when they neared the dropping zone. They crouched there, strapped in their harnesses, parachute static lines clipped to the rail, like guard dogs on leash. The line would twitch the chute out of its package and then, as one hurtled earthwards, the line would snap under one's weight.

Charlie would jump first. To him it was nothing, "a piece of cake". Then Rick, then Blair. *He*'d jumped many times before, visiting Resistance groups in France.

Rick wished he had had more practice. But in those few weeks since his London interview there'd been so much else to learn. Among other things, his cover story. It wasn't enough to dress up and be fitted out with false documents. You had to create for yourself a whole personality, so that you could play your part and answer any question without hesitating.

Rick went over his own story yet again. He was Ricardo Calvino, orphaned when an RAF bomb

21

flattened his home, now trying to trace his aunt, whose surname he wasn't sure of, because she'd just married again.

Blair was Alessandro Morelli. Businessman from the North, the part of Italy Blair knew best, from trade fairs he'd attended in peacetime at Turin and Milan and Genoa.

Charlie Morgan had been the main problem. He could never pass for an Italian. He knew only a few phrases. There were hardly any men in the British forces as fluent as Blair and Rick. To find one who was also an expert wireless operator would have been a needle-in-a-haystack job. But the technical skill was essential – and the training lengthy.

Charlie himself had solved the difficulty. "Suppose I'm Hungarian?" he had suggested to the clever men in Baker Street. "They're on Hitler's side."

"But you can't speak Hungarian!"

"Who can, outside Hungary?"

"But you'd have to talk in *some* language..."

"I'll talk Welsh." Charlie had grinned triumphantly at his interviewers. "How many Italians know Welsh? Or can tell it from Hungarian? Can *you*, gentlemen?"

That floored them. They had to send him. There was no better "pianist" available. Charlie became Anton Karády from Budapest.

Now it was his voice that called Rick back to the present. "Won't be long now. Must be running up the Adriatic coast."

They could see nothing. But Rick had studied the map endlessly and he could picture the pale sheen of the sea, the humpy line of the Apennines with their gulfs of inky shadow and upthrust fangs of moonlit rock. And close to the shore there'd be the steely gleam of the railway running straight southwards to Bari and Brindisi.

There'd been discussions earlier, Blair had told him – should they be landed on the west coast by a sub? That would have meant a much longer overland trek to Sant'Arpino, with greater risk of capture.

The east coast offered a shorter route. But the Navy did not want to hazard a submarine in the enclosed waters of the Adriatic, so it must be a parachute drop. The RAF, in turn, had not cared for the idea of making that drop blind, without guidance from the ground, in the rough mountain country above Sant'Arpino. Charlie had explained the snags.

"They like to come in low, about six hundred feet – and that's dicey when you've got crags sticking up all over the place. But it's not just the risk of pranging the aircraft – they do spare a thought for the blokes they're dropping. No sense in landing one of us in a treetop and another of us half-way down the face of a precipice."

Rick had agreed wholeheartedly.

"Or dropping my box of tricks down a bottomless ravine!" Charlie went on. "If *that* goes missing, the whole show's a wash-out."

So the drop would have to be in the narrow coastal strip where the land was flat. Once safely down, they would have to move fast during the remaining hours of darkness, heading for the safety of the hills. Luckily the area was thinly populated and, being so remote from any fighting zone, should be free of patrolling troops and sentries. And the only important highway ran parallel with the railway, hugging the coast, so that they would not have to cross it. They would be dropped on the inland side and would merely have to get across a few miles of countryside to reach the mountains.

And then, Rick told himself as he huddled there in the darkness, I shall have to justify my existence. *I'm* the one who's supposed to know the hills.

Even Blair would depend on him. It was a rather alarming thought. But exhilarating.

Suddenly the red light flashed. Someone was drawing aside the hatch covering that ominous hole. A voice asked, "Ready?" Charlie was shuffling forward on his behind, gripping the rim of the opening, thrusting his legs down into the racing shimmer of moonlight.

Rick braced himself to follow. Speed was vital. One second intervals. A wasted second meant hundreds of yards between you and the man who'd jumped before.

Now the green light. "Go!" grunted the dispatcher. Charlie went. Rick dangled momentarily in the void. "GO!" A hand shoved. He was on his way.

FOUR

The sickening moments of headlong fall ended with the reassuring tug of his harness as the parachute opened. More slowly now, the pallid landscape rose to meet him.

Even so, dropping from this low altitude, he'd little chance to study it. To his right the ruffled silver of the sea, the glint of rails, the pale ribbon of the road... below him the little winding river they were aiming for, lined with poplars like gigantic cats' tails... A wayward air current twirled him about and he saw Charlie's parachute crumpled on the ground.

He made a pretty fair landing, he thought, rolled over with a gasp of relief and began to unbuckle his harness. In no time the sergeant was looming over him.

"OK, boy-o?"

Charlie did not bother about the "sir". In this moment of stress, rank did not seem important.

"Fine, thanks." Rick struggled to his feet. "Where's the major?"

"Over there. And the container further on. I saw it come down."

"Thank God for that!"

The fourth parachute had carried all their equipment – most importantly Charlie's case with the radio transmitter. Without that, they would have no contact with headquarters.

They picked their way across the river-bed, now in July almost dried up. Moonlight gleamed on shallow pools, but mostly it was a litter of smooth boulders, pale as cheeses. A good place, for the moment, to dump their bundled parachutes.

Blair reached the container first. Swiftly they unpacked it and distributed the contents. Rick was to carry his share in an old Italian army pack with shoulder straps. It reminded him of a hike he'd made in the Lake District with a school friend. He was sorry for Charlie with that suitcase, compact-looking but heavy. The essential radio was the new SOE model, the B2, but it still weighed about thirty pounds.

"Now," said Blair briskly, "we must get rid of this gear." After a quick glance round to check that they had gathered up everything, he led the way back to the shelter of the river-bed. The container and its kapok packing, the rolled-up parachutes and their harnesses, were sunk, well weighted with stones, in the deepest pool they could see. In a few days, no doubt, some goatherd would spot them and haul them out. He might – or might not – report his find to the authorities. But long before then, the trio should be safe in the hills and their trail would be cold.

There was more danger — immediate danger — if the low-flying Halifax had been reported as suspicious. But the air crew would have done their best to disguise the object of their mission, for, having dropped their passengers, they were going on to scatter propaganda leaflets over the area. Some were sure to be handed in to the police, who were used to leaflet raids but not, in this region at least, to parachutists.

Blair glanced at his watch. "Fine. But we'll have to get cracking."

The river-bed stretched before them, clear in the light of the sinking moon. They had reckoned on it for good cover — winter floods had gouged out a deep channel, creating high banks screened and shadowed by trees and bushes — and it was an obvious route to the hills. But it could be time-wasting too, for it ran anything but straight and it was hard not to slither and stumble noisily on the loose stones. Fortunately they had seen no sign of habitation. This was poor farming country. And the Italians, Rick remembered, liked to cluster sociably in villages, not scatter their farms and cottages all over the landscape as the British did. Only once did they hear a dog bark and that, Charlie muttered, was a good mile away.

"We'll make faster time on the top," said Blair. So they climbed the bank and flitted along beneath the poplars. The going was easier on the sparse grass and sun-baked earth. Also, they could cut corners when the river developed too many zigzags. But just as they were congratulating themselves on their quicker progress, they were startled by the sound of a train.

"Down!" Blair grunted, and flung himself into the dappled shadow of a thorn bush.

The clicketty-click of the train grew louder. They must be quite close to the track, thought Rick with dismay. Much closer than they should have been. The track ran straight along the low Adriatic shore. So, walking fast, they ought by now to be a couple of miles away.

They weren't. Raising his head cautiously he saw the grey length of blacked-out coaches gliding along the top of a low embankment only a few hundred yards to the right.

"Lucky that didn't come along a bit earlier," Charlie murmured in his ear. "Driver couldn't have missed us drifting down. Not with this moon!"

The train rattled away southwards towards Brindisi. There was no doubt that this was the main line. Rick knew from his study of the map. No town big enough this side of the Apennines, no industry to justify a branch line.

He said so to Blair as they stood up again. "Oh, there's no mix-up of railway tracks," agreed the major irritably. "We've been dropped by the wrong river, that's all!"

"Hell of a lot of these rivers," said Charlie. He too had studied the map before they started. Every mile or two there seemed to be a fine blue thread running down from the mountain range, across the narrow coastal strip and into the sea. "Hard to spot a particular one from the air when you've no landmarks or signal lights to guide you." He said it defensively, a loyal RAF man, alone with two Army types, both senior in rank.

"All the rivers come down off the same hills." Rick tried to strike a soothing note.

"But some come straighter than others," snapped Blair. "We've been walking north instead of west. Look

28

at the stars – needn't waste more time on maps and compasses! I remember this river. Does a right-angle bend, runs almost parallel with the coast, then twists the other way to reach the sea." He hesitated briefly. "Best stick to it now, though. It'll lead us up into the hills not far from the one we want. Cost us an hour, though. We'll have to get a move on."

The next few miles were going to be the trickiest. Rick had no illusions about that. People would soon be stirring, with the approach of dawn. They would not be able to bypass all the inhabited places, but the further inland they could get, unobserved, the better it would be.

To his relief the river-bed now took a purposeful bend to the west. At last it was leading them in the right direction, away from the railway and the coastal road. The mountains loomed vaguely in front, the moon just sinking behind them. It was the darkest hour before the dawn. They could just see to stumble along beneath the fringe of trees.

Soon, though, a backward glance showed a warning tinge of pink in the eastern sky. A cock crowed. Another answered it. Before long the sun would be shooting up out of the sea behind them.

Blair, stalking in front, dropped down into the sunken water-course, beckoning them to follow. "We're a wee bit conspicuous now," he grunted.

They hurried after him, crunching over drifts of pebbles, splashing through the cold shallows, watching for unsteady boulders underfoot. Inevitably it would slow them down somewhat, but they dared no longer show themselves on the top of the bank.

The long wall of the Apennines stretched in front, wreathed in tattered scarves of dirty white cloud. Ominously a few spots of rain pattered down.

"Damn," said Blair softly. He was not referring to the weather. "I think we've hit on the one river that flows slap through a village."

Somewhere ahead a clock was striking. Dogs barked. More cocks crowed. An early motorcyclist went chugging through the dank morning.

They came to a bridge, stone-built and massive, arching high above their heads. Shadowy, screened by bushes, the arch at least offered excellent cover, while they considered their next move.

Thankfully they squatted under it, though the river-bed was thick with household rubbish and worse. "Obviously," said Blair, "we're approaching civilization!"

Women's voices, animated and vibrant, pierced the damp air. There must be houses overlooking the river. Strangers would be noticeable at this early hour. Better not show themselves until more people were moving about.

"This must be Santo Stefano," said Rick. "We should have been two miles further south."

Though Santo Stefano lay outside the mountain area he knew best, he did remember a visit in some professor's car. There had been an old church, which at fourteen he had found boring. And he recalled the bridge under which they were now sheltering.

Heavy footsteps went clumping overhead, the unhurried steps of countrymen. There were shouts of greeting, then conversation. A glowing cigarette end curved through the air, followed by another. The voices merged into a continuous babble.

The men must be leaning on the parapet. He caught the word *autobus*. That explained everything: there was a bus-stop directly above them. He listened keenly, then reported to his companions. "They'll soon be gone. They're waiting for a bus. To Roncolo."

"Roncolo?" said Blair. "On our way! Pity we can't..."

"You're telling me," muttered Charlie.

The men on the bridge must be smoking like chimneys. The rank smoke drifted down on the eddies of a sluggish breeze. Blair evidently thought it safe to risk a cigarette himself. Foul as the cheap tobacco was, it satisfied his craving.

He had time only for a few puffs. There was a slither of boots on the rough bank outside, a rustle of foliage thrust aside. Blair stubbed out his cigarette. They all stiffened, staring at the semicircle of clammy white daylight framed by the arch. Into that frame dropped a grey figure, a silhouette that froze and stood peering at them, letting out a startled exclamation.

There was no point now in keeping silent. Blair called out, in a matter-of-fact tone, *"Buon giorno!"*

FIVE

The quiet "good morning" seemed to reassure the stranger.

"*Buon giorno, signori!*" he answered politely. He turned his back, fumbling with buttons. So, thought Rick thankfully, there was no cause for alarm. The boy was younger than himself. His abrupt arrival had the most natural of reasons.

Best to follow Blair's lead, pass some further casual remark, to disarm suspicion and explain their own presence under the bridge and deliberately drop into the local idiom he'd picked up from the Sant'Arpino lads. That would suggest that he came from these parts and was no mysterious stranger. So he called out, chattily, "We're dodging the rain."

"It's leaving off, now," said the boy over his shoulder. "Bus is due – if you want it." He ran, scrabbling up the bank.

Blair did not hesitate. "We'd better go," he murmured, "or some busybody will start rumours of sinister characters lurking under the bridge."

Rick's heart quickened its beat as he followed the major. This was the first testing moment. But it had to come sooner or later.

A number of men were clustered at the end of the bridge. There were several women too, aproned and shawled, laden with baskets of produce, one containing a live – and lively – hen. Heads turned at the new arrivals. There were civil murmurs of "*Buon giorno, signori*" and some inquisitive stares.

Charlie stood a little apart. That general tactic had been agreed beforehand. Charlie, with his suitcase, was the most vulnerable member of the party. If it had to be opened, disclosing its suspicious contents, he'd have only two choices – run or risk arrest. Blair and Rick would help him if they could, but not at the price of being caught themselves, which would mean the end of the whole mission. So, in a situation like the present, they would behave as if they did not know him.

Fortunately the bus came clattering down the street and pulled up, wheezing and juddering, while everyone crowded aboard.

Blair held out some crumpled notes and asked for two return tickets to Roncolo. Returns seemed somehow more respectable than singles. They suggested a fixed address.

The bus was crammed now, but they found seats together. Blair plunged into earnest conversation with Rick. "I was telling you about my unfortunate nephew

33

in Turin. It is a long story..."

It was. Blair made sure of that. Rick got the idea at once and played up to him. Had they sat in silence their fellow passengers would have leant forward and started to chat. But their natural good manners would prevent any of them, however curious, from interrupting the flow of Blair's narrative.

Rick, for his part, continued to indicate that, though Blair was a city man from the north, he himself belonged to this region. An odd word, a local reference, would establish him as a native, but the less talk he had with the real natives the safer it would be.

Charlie, three rows in front of them, seemed all right – if all right was a fair description of being wedged against an enormous peasant granny, nursing the basket which contained the obstreperous hen. The bird constantly threatened to escape. What with clamorous protests and the woman's repeated apologies for its misbehaviour, Charlie had little chance to show his ignorance of Italian. Rick heard him manage a reassuring "*Non importa*!" and a courteous "*Prego*!" and this seemed to satisfy her, for she turned and addressed a strident monologue to her friends.

Rick felt that things were going remarkably well.

It was a risk, travelling by bus, but it would save them miles of walking and the probably greater risks of other encounters. Eventually they would have to mix openly with the inhabitants. Better to take the plunge and get it over.

The sun broke through. They were getting nearer to the comparative safety of the mountains. The green foothills rose with their neat vine terraces, their dangling grapes. There were more women trudging with heaped baskets, a cart with white oxen, an old priest wobbling on an equally venerable bicycle... Shrill-voiced crop-headed little boys ran and scuffled... all in the uniform of the Balilla, Mussolini's substitute for Cubs and Scouts.

A road sign said RONCOLO. An avenue of cypresses spread long black shadows – ill omen, like prison bars! – across the dusty white roadway. To right and left the houses began to close in. The bus drew up in a wide piazza where stall-holders were setting up trestle-tables under the plane trees. Rick's mouth watered at the sight of mounds of oranges. He mustn't show that in Britain he'd seen no such abundance for the last four years.

"Coffee, I think," Blair murmured, looking across to a white-aproned man wiping some tables in the shade. "Let our fellow passengers disperse." A good idea, thought Rick. Someone might be curious to see where these strangers were going. Better to leave them guessing. Also, after that forced night-march, the very notion of coffee was enticing.

A policeman was watching the bus unload. Rick noted with relief that he wore the white summer uniform and crested helmet of the local force. He was not one of the much more formidable Carabinieri who also patrolled these rural areas. However, he was staring hard at Charlie. With dismay Rick saw him put out a detaining hand.

He could only follow Blair to the café table. The major was already fumbling for a cigarette. Glancing back, Rick saw that the policeman was pointing to the suitcase. Charlie was shaking his head, protesting volubly in – presumably – Welsh, and indicating that he did not understand Italian. The policeman grew more menacing.

Man to man, the sergeant could have eaten him for

breakfast. As for the pistol in its little holster, the Italian would never have had a chance to draw it. But it wasn't just man to man. One false move by Charlie, in this public place, and he'd be done for and their whole mission would be in jeopardy.

Rick looked anxiously at Blair across the table. Silently he mouthed the words, what can we do? The major shook his head. "He's a crafty one."

Rick strained his ears to catch what was being said a few yards away.

"I asked you, signore, what you have in this case."

"Excuse please, I do not well understand Italian."

"Ah! Then your passport?"

Charlie groped in his inside pocket, gabbling indignant Welsh, and fished out the document.

Seeing the Hungarian crest the policeman became slightly less bullying.

"Comrades," pleaded Charlie. "Allies – Germany, Italy, Hungary."

The policeman opened the passport and suddenly became almost amiable. Rick could see that a loose piece of paper had been slipped inside, the ham so to speak in the sandwich. It looked like a five hundred lire note. Good money for a low-paid local policeman.

This one seemed to think so. With the deftness of a conjuror he extracted the note, returned the passport, raised his hand in salute and strolled away.

Without a glance at his friends, Charlie took a seat at the next table.

The coffee was not very good. To Rick, remembering those bygone breakfasts at the Tre Corone in Sant' Arpino, this ersatz concoction of acorns or dandelions was a disappointment. But as a hot drink, served with rolls crisp from the bakehouse, it was welcome enough.

He found himself relaxing slightly in the growing warmth of the morning, watching the busy life around him. How *good* to be in Italy again! Happy memories washed round him. Then he pulled himself up sharply. He could not, *must* not relax. The bus ride had passed off safely, Charlie had neatly evaded the policeman, but there was still danger all around them, every second they remained here.

This was still Mussolini's Italy, a country at war with his own. On the other side of the square the chattering boys of the Balilla were forming into their ranks. In their little black hats, Blair commented in an acid undertone, they looked like monkeys. Solemn eight-year-olds were saluting their self-important ten-year-old leaders. Now they were chanting in unison the Ten Commandments of Fascism...

"*Mussolini ha sempre ragione...*"

"Mussolini is always right." That was what the Fascists taught the children, almost from the cradle. They sought to produce a completely brainwashed generation. The Balilla must inform even against their own parents if they heard disloyal talk at home. How zestfully would these young monkeys denounce a British agent if they scented one!

No, Rick told himself, never relax. Danger everywhere.

Blair leant across the table. "Which way, when we leave here? You're the navigator now."

Rick was only too well aware of that. They were pretty near where they had aimed to be, only a couple of hours behind schedule. He needed no map to remind him. Another of those mountain rivers flowed down through this town. A mule track climbed parallel with it, continuing over a pass to another valley beyond. He

37

took a piece of paper and began to draw a simple sketch. There was a protesting grunt from Blair and Rick looked up to see the sandy eyebrows knitted in disapproval.

"No need —"

"Not for you." Taking his courage in both hands Rick finished his map. "For our — 'pianist'." He glanced meaningly at Charlie, who was observing them covertly but unable to understand what was said. "He will need guidance when we go – he will have to follow our... music."

Blair nodded imperceptibly. He took the point.

Rick let the sketch lie on the table. When they rose to leave, he brushed it with his sleeve so that it fluttered across to fall almost at Charlie's feet. Charlie dived to pick it up. "*Signore!*"

Rick was already some yards away. He turned, gestured that he did not want the paper. "*Grazie, signore! Non fa niente.*"

Charlie shrugged, crumpled the sketch and dropped it casually beside his cup. Rick felt sure, however, that when the proprietor came to clear the tables he would not find it there.

SIX

They dawdled some minutes in the piazza, so that Charlie would not be seen to hurry after them. Rick bought half a kilo of delicious peaches, a long crusty loaf and a length of salami. From another stall Blair chose a flask of dark red wine.

Soon the market hubbub faded behind them. Tall biscuit-coloured houses gave place to the silvery shimmer of olive trees, the green regiments of terraced vines. The paved road became a dusty track with shallow steps to ease the gradient. An occasional walnut tree flung a splash of shade. Rick felt the sun fierce on his shoulders. Under the old army pack the shirt clung damply to his skin.

Peasants paused in their work to shout a greeting.

Mainly Blair left it to Rick to answer. Unwise to offend these people in their friendly curiosity. Equally unwise to get involved. Mostly the peasants were some distance from the track — a wave and a word were enough to satisfy them. Only one, a young fellow repairing a stone wall at the roadside, was more persistent. To Blair, just then walking in front, he touched his cap respectfully, but to Rick he said frankly, "A hot day for a mountain journey! Where are you heading then?"

Rick shrugged. "Who knows?" He lowered his voice and nodded towards Blair's receding back. "It is for *him* to say." He lowered his voice even more. "He is very important."

"So?" The young man's eyes widened. "He looks it. He is perhaps from the government?"

"Most certainly."

The wall-builder spat in the dust. Respect and hatred mingled in the gesture. "Then I ask no questions," he said. "Important persons from the government are everywhere. But if he is searching for oil in these mountains he will be unlucky. If he is looking for tax-dodgers he may be luckier." And, pleased with his own joke, he let Rick walk by and the clunk of his wall-building was resumed. Another awkward moment had been passed. Rick breathed again.

He could only hope that Charlie, in his turn, would get by without arousing suspicions. But the Welshman had already shown himself a wily bird, quick to meet emergencies. Charlie, with his ignorance of Italian, had his own defence against prying questions. The wall-builder would probably assume that he was some lowly assistant of the important government personage who had just passed by and would wave him on up the hill. Even the suitcase would fit in and help to explain why

Charlie had dropped behind.

But it would be a relief to get beyond these orchards and vineyards into the forest whose treetops now beckoned encouragingly from the next crest.

Until then, this peaceful landscape was altogether too deceptive. Rick's thoughts flew back to the English countryside he had just left, with its constant reminders of the war — chirpy little Land Girls driving huge tractors, signposts with names removed since 1940 to puzzle the expected Nazi invaders, farm wagons left in the middle of fields to obstruct the landing of enemy gliders, tank-traps, concrete pill-boxes everywhere...

Nothing like that here. The peasants were going quietly about their work as if they had never heard of Hitler or Stalin, Churchill or Roosevelt. But they had. Their blaring radio, their ranting Mussolini never let them forget the war. Their innocent curiosity, their love of gossip made it dangerous to be a passing stranger.

At last the forest fringe! And no further encounters. Thankfully the two men plunged into the cool shade of the oaks and chestnuts and flung themselves down in a hollow some distance aside from the track. There, if they kept quiet, they would be invisible to anyone passing by, but could watch out for Charlie. And sure enough, about ten minutes later, he caught up with them, answering their quiet call.

"Any more problems?" Blair asked.

"No, sir."

"Nasty moment with that cop in the square."

"Oh, I know his sort. Spotted my case, probably thought I was working the black market. Now he's sure of it! But he believes in live-and-let-live."

"I wouldn't try it on the Carabinieri, though," Rick warned him. He explained the difference between the two police forces. The Carabinieri weren't local constables. They were really part of the army, a crack mounted corps, smart and proud of their reputation. "They're not saints," said Rick, "but think twice before you offer them money."

Now they had reached the shelter of the forest, Blair decided that they should lie low for a few hours, get some much-needed rest and avoid the risk of meeting other users of the track. They sliced up the loaf and the salami. The sausage was powerfully seasoned. It was unlikely to smell any more appetising as the day wore on. The wine was passed round, but they drank sparingly. "Still got to keep our wits about us," said Blair. He lit a cigarette.

It was safe now to open Charlie's case and study the map. Rick's forefinger traced the thread of river up from the town they had left, through the forest, until it reached the open mountains. There, like the stem of some uprooted plant, it broke into several fine blue lines, branching out and ending at the source from which each sprang.

"Sant'Arpino." Blair pointed to the town in another valley to the north.

"Yes, sir. But I suggest we make for *here*, first." Rick moved his finger on over the uplands, coming to rest at a high point near the head of a wooded valley leading down to the place that was their eventual destination. "There's a shepherd's hut. Old Andrea Alberti used to bring his sheep up here in the summer. We could shelter there for tonight."

"What if the man's there?"

"He'd be all right. He was a nice old boy. We used to be real friends."

"There's a war on," Charlie reminded him.

"He'd never give *me* away."

"But what about us?" Blair demanded.

"You're friends of mine."

"If he turns awkward," said Charlie, "we'd just have to make sure..." He did not finish the sentence. Rick felt a chill shudder. He knew that SOE work left no room for sentiment. Could he drag poor old Andrea into this? But he must now. Too late to change plans. He felt sure that if they ran into the shepherd he could be trusted not to give them away. But Blair and Charlie were hard-bitten cynical men. They might be forgiven for thinking that he was naive.

The midday heat penetrated even the green shade. "What's that noise?" Charlie asked. "Sort of whirring. Goes on all the time."

"Oh, the cicadas," Rick explained. The incessant sound of the insects was a part of his Italian summer memories. Long afternoons, leading on to soft velvety evenings with nightingales singing in the Castle gardens... Even today, for all his tension, for all his anxious calculations he had to fight against drowsiness.

Blair glanced at his watch. "Might as well make up some sleep," he said. He turned to Charlie. "You take first spell on guard, sergeant. Wake me in, let's see, an hour and a half."

"Very good, sir."

Blair stretched himself out, closed his eyes and with the self-discipline of long experience seemed almost immediately to pass into unconsciousness. Rick, head pillowed on his pack, tried to do the same and feared for a minute or two that he would never manage it. But it had been a long night and a long walk, and the food and wine helped. The next thing he felt was Blair gently shaking his arm.

"Your turn, Rick."

They had left him to the last. Charlie was curled up, dead to the world. Blair had obviously just finished his own stint of watching, but showed no immediate eagerness to lie down again. They talked together in low voices.

"I'm going to find this a wee bit strange," Blair murmured.

"Strange, sir?"

"Ay. In France we'd folk all round us. Germans – specially the Gestapo – and French collaborators who'd turn us over to them... But *here*..."

"Shouldn't be so bad," Rick suggested.

The major's reaction was almost irritable. "I don't want a rest-cure. But I do want to get something done. It was no picnic in France, but at least you knew where you were and what you could do. There was a network. They were waiting to welcome you when you dropped. Told you just how you could help." He sounded wistful. "There were clear objectives. Bridges to blow, trains to sabotage, buildings to burn."

"There's all that here, sir. And if there *is* a resistance group starting up —"

"We've got to locate it. Then find just what it can do. We've had it too cushy today. I've a nasty feeling..."

"In what way, sir?"

"We've seen one village cop so far. No troops, no signs of military activity. What did we pass on that bus ride? Damn all. This area looks to me like a backwater. There may be damn all for us to do. Oh, well, better try to get some more sleep, I suppose." He extinguished his cigarette carefully. "We'd best be on our way in an hour. Wake me – if I *need* waking." He lay down again.

Rick had never seen Blair in so black a mood. No doubt his heart was really in the more promising activities of the French Resistance. Did he resent being taken out of them to mount this rather dubious little mission to an obscure area in Italy? No doubt his fluency in the language had landed him with the Arpino Assignment. There was such a shortage of Italian-speaking officers. So the powers-that-be had transferred him, willy-nilly, just as they had plucked Rick himself out of his training camp. No one else to send.

They could only hope that they would not be wasting their time on a wild-goose chase.

For himself, of course, it was different. Though he had been born in England, grown up and gone to school there – had thought of himself as English first and foremost – he had always been proud of his mixed blood, the Italian heritage on his mother's side. For four whole years, since 1939 – too long – he had been cut off from his Italian roots. It was wonderful to be in Italy again, even under these bizarre conditions with all their dangers and disadvantages. Brought back, oddly enough, by the very war that had cut the link. And how wonderful it would be if his strange mission helped to shorten this tragic conflict between his parents' two countries! He felt a moment of romantic exaltation at the thought. His mother would have been shattered by this war. At least he was now trying to do something to end it. If only she had lived and knew what he was striving to achieve, how pleased she would have been!

From this reverie (Was he being sentimental, the matter-of-fact English side of his nature demanded?) he was abruptly brought back to hard reality.

Harness jingled... Measured hoofbeats sounded from the beaten track some fifty yards away... Voices... More than one rider... Coming *down*...

He stiffened. Their resting-place had been carefully chosen with just such a possibility in mind. Blair and Charlie seemed fast asleep in the bottom of the hollow. Safer not to disturb them, lest in waking they made some sound to reveal their presence. He would be all right himself if he kept his head down and peeped cautiously through the undergrowth.

There were only two riders. Rick got a good view, for they were big men, sitting straight in the saddle and on fine chargers whose proud heads moved high above the screening foliage. He recognized the uniform of the Carabinieri. How often had he stood as a schoolboy, waiting on the street corner in Sant'Arpino, to watch the well-groomed glossy horses emerge from the archway at the Carabinieri headquarters on one of their routine patrols! Now – if they but knew of his existence – these elegant policemen would be remorselessly hunting that boy who had once admired them.

It was not a comfortable thought. But, once the two riders had passed safely down the track and every sound of them had faded, there was a wry consolation to be gained. When Rick roused his companions half an hour later he was able to tell Blair, with a grin, "Things may not be so cushy after all." He reported how nearly they had missed an encounter with the Carabinieri patrol. "They were heading downhill, sir. So that should mean we aren't likely to run into a patrol when we get out on to the open mountain."

"Let's hope your wall-building friend has knocked off work for today – and the chaps you've just seen don't talk to anyone else we passed as we came up this morning. They might start wondering why *they* never saw three mysterious strangers. Suppose they decide to turn round and come back to look for us, just to be on the safe side?"

Blair's question reminded Rick that the major, though highly intelligent, was essentially a man of the city, not, like Rick, country-bred. Probably Blair had never been on a horse. Even if he had, it was unlikely that he had ever ridden one for miles through wild areas like the Apennines.

"I don't think they would, sir," he suggested tactfully. "They're given a route to patrol. I mean, a horse isn't like a motorbike. You can't just turn it round and add another twenty miles to the day's mileage. If they did hear about us and wonder who we were, they'd only be able to report it when they got back to base. By which time..." He shrugged.

Blair seemed satisfied. And apparently cheered by the near miss while he had slept. The adrenalin was flowing again, thought Rick. Blair needed the stimulus of danger.

They set off, following the upward track, alert for unexpected encounters, ready to seek cover if necessary. The woodland thinned as they climbed higher. Finally they emerged upon an utterly different landscape, open mountain, bleak and arid as the moon, sloping up to the sky with a brown and blue backdrop of savage peaks. But when they got over the crest, the scenery changed again into something slightly less desolate. Between the rock slabs and the drifts of clinking shale were stretches of green pasture.

There were sheep now. First one tiny blob moving across the wilderness, then two, three... sudden little bubbles of movement against a background of utter stillness without any other flicker of life. The tinkle of sheep-bells came faintly through the thin air.

Rick stopped. "You can't see the hut, sir," he whispered. "It's down in that dip. Will you wait here while I go forward and recce?"

"Do that." The two others sat down among the rocks.

Rick stole forward. Everything looked just as he remembered it. Soon he sighted the roughly-built cabin standing beside the runnel of cold spring water that never quite dried up.

Someone was there. Smoke drifted from the chimney, grey-white in the shadowy hollow, turning orange as it rose into the slanting rays of the setting sun.

Would it be Andrea Alberti? To Rick, at fourteen, the grey-bearded shepherd had seemed incredibly old, a marvel of ancient vigour striding along the Apennine ridges. But at fourteen, even forty seemed old. These peasants seemed to live for ever. With luck he might still be Rick's friend.

A dog barked. Went on barking. Furiously. A stooping figure straightened up from the streamlet, kettle in hand. It *was* Alberti. He advanced slowly, shading his eyes against the glare.

The dog raced ahead. It halted twenty paces from Rick, snarling, every hair on end.

He had never known this dog, nor had it known him. Some of these brutes could be ferocious. He shouted, "Call him off, Andrea! It's only me."

The old man let out a cry of amazement. "Silence, Pepito! It is a friend. God bless us, it's the English signorino!"

SEVEN

Andrea was hugging him, the bristly cheek like sand-paper against his own. Then the shepherd stood back and studied him.

"You have grown, my boy!"

Rick laughed. "It is four years!"

"So long? Ah, this accursed war..." The bright eyes clouded. "But how did you come? We are at war with England. A terrible, wicked mistake. Our countries have always been such friends. Still, they have allowed you to come here..."

"Hardly *allowed*! In fact, if you tell anyone —"

"What do you take me for? Enemies – you and I? Explain this miracle. As if you had dropped from the skies!"

"That is exactly what I have done." He explained about the parachute. "I am a soldier now."

"So? Everywhere it is the same. They are sending mere boys to die – in Africa, in Greece, in Russia, worst of all! One of my own grandsons, frozen to death there…"

"Oh, I *am* sorry, Andrea."

"It is that Hitler. He has dragged Italy into this madness. And our marvellous Mussolini allowed him!" The old man turned aside and spat contemptuously. "I tell you, Ricardo, I pray now for the English and the Americans to win this war and waken us from the nightmare. I am not the only one who says this."

This was encouraging. Rick felt it was safe to confide in the old man. There was a senior British officer with him, he explained. Their mission was to help the Italian people get out of the mess in which their dictator had landed them.

Rick shouted to his companions. They came hurrying down from their hiding-place among the rocks. Pepito exploded into a frenzy of barking and rushed to the attack. But before Andrea could call him off he had been pacified by Charlie, who seemed to possess some mysterious gift for communication. The dog was soon frisking round him with the utmost friendliness.

Rick made introductions. "This is my old friend Andrea Alberti, sir. Andrea, this is Major Blair. And Sergeant Morgan of the Royal Air Force."

"I fought beside the British in the other war," announced the shepherd proudly. "The Tommies! They came to help us against the Austrians. 1917! We were on the same side, then – we should be now."

He bowed them into his hut, apologizing for its smallness and simplicity. But, such as it was, it was at their disposal. They should be safe enough here. Often a week could pass without his seeing a stranger.

Rick felt a surge of relief. He had successfully fulfilled his first task. He had got the party to a place where Charlie could hide his radio and operate it when needed. No longer had they to run the gauntlet of inquisitive eyes with that embarrassing but indispensable item of equipment. Outside the hut there were a dozen places where the transmitter could be concealed among the rocks when not in use.

Charlie lost no time in stowing it away. But first he unpacked the map and handed round the pistols. They were neat little Italian-made Berettas, of the improved 1935 model, as used by the Italian armed services and police, seven cartridges capacity. Rick felt better as he felt the hardness of the gun against his body. They were no longer in the market place at Roncolo. Up here, in the lonely spaces of the mountains, they would have a fair chance to fight back if they were challenged.

Andrea saw the pistols. Blair made sure he did. "If things go wrong," he warned the shepherd, "you would be asked why you gave us shelter. You can say you had no choice. We had guns and threatened you."

Andrea smiled. "You have guns," he echoed. "You threaten me. I am terrified, major." He pottered about, spreading sheepskins for them to sit on and stirring a saucepan over the fire.

He enquired after Rick's father. He had a deep respect for the learning of *il dottore* Weston, who used to come and work with the professors from Rome on their excavation of the ancient villa. He was eager, too, to know how the war was really going.

"Our newspapers!" he cried scornfully. "Our broadcasts! I think they tell us only lies."

Rick told him of the Allied successes in Sicily. As he spoke, he glanced across at Blair, silent, puffing at one of his appalling cigarettes. He could guess what the Scot was pondering. He was assessing Andrea. Was this talkative old peasant to be trusted? Or would he seek favour with the Fascist authorities – maybe claim a few thousand lire as a reward – by seizing the first chance to betray his guests?

Rick, for his own part, would have staked his life on Andrea's integrity. But, he had to remind himself, Blair was in charge – and it was his duty to take every precaution. Blair's experience of life was quite different from his own. Much longer, too. In Italy – before the war – Blair had mixed not with simple shepherds but with smart operators in the cut-throat world of business. He must have learnt to watch out for every trick, to be sceptical always, to be hard. Now, as an agent, he kept to the same rules.

After all, Rick admitted to himself, what was their own operation but one long deception? Disguises, cover stories, forged papers, *lies*. How could they complain if the same weapons were used against them? And yet – and *yet* – he could not believe that Andrea would betray them.

Even Blair seemed satisfied. When their host went out for a moment to fetch more firewood, he murmured in English, "You seem to have found us the right man."

"Glad you agree, sir." Rick felt much happier.

"He may not be able to tell us much himself – but he could lead us to contacts."

Andrea had heard of damage done to the railway. "Sabotage – that is the word, signori? The police caught no one. It is said that the men came from the hills. Communists, say some. Perhaps. In Sant'Arpino we take little interest in politics. Or it might be army deserters. There are many of those, now that we seem to be losing the war."

Blair brightened. The railway. The coastal railway, a life-line for military operations in the South. That was one useful objective for SOE activity.

Andrea insisted on their sharing his stew. In return, he helped them to finish the salami and the peaches and to empty the flagon of wine. He accepted enthusiastically one of Blair's cigarettes.

Charlie went out to his suitcase and was soon running an aerial up the stone chimney-stack outside. It would be quite inconspicuous unless someone was searching for such a thing.

"Should be OK, sir. Course, you never know about reception in the mountains until you try."

Andrea was fascinated. He asked Rick, "Will he talk to London now?"

"It's not quite so simple, Andrea. He can't 'talk' like the men you hear on the ordinary radio. He can only send messages in Morse – dot, dot, dash, dash – that sort of thing."

"Ah, code? That I understand."

"And he can't send them to London because of the distance. This set isn't powerful enough. He can send only to one place – the station allotted to him." Rick took care not to say where it was.

"Of course," said Andrea sagely. "It was so with the carrier pigeons in the other war."

"And he can't send a message yet – it must be done each night at a fixed time."

"So? Patience is a great thing! Who should know that, if not a shepherd?"

Blair was already scribbling a brief report on their safe arrival. It was another two hours before Charlie's practised fingers could begin tapping it out on the transmitter. They all kept silent so as not to distract him. Andrea seemed to imagine that any noise they made would be audible at the receiving station. Rick thought it best not to muddle him with technical explanations.

"He looks skilful, your sergeant," said Andrea admiringly when Charlie closed his suitcase. "Does he never make mistakes with these dots and dashes?"

"Never." It was simpler not to say that Charlie always made two mistakes, but deliberate ones. The receiving station must have proof that the message was genuine and from the agent concerned, not a false one from an enemy who had penetrated the system. Early in each message Charlie must include an intentional error, the "bluff". And to confirm that it *was* intentional, not accidental, he must later in the message make a second mistake, the "true check". The two mistakes would show beyond doubt that it was the agent transmitting, not an enemy.

Charlie went out into the darkness and stowed the set in its hiding-place. Even on this desolate mountain, one must stick closely to the rules.

"So," said Andrea, "they will know that you have arrived safely and are with friends. A wonderful invention."

"Better than carrying pigeons around," said Rick.

But they could not be certain yet that their message had been picked up. Charlie had two pre-arranged times every day, one for outward transmissions, the other for receiving the acknowledgement and any fresh instructions. It would be after midnight before he could stand by and hope for the reply.

Long before then the others had settled down for some much-needed sleep. There was little space to spare in the tiny hut when they stretched out under Andrea's sheepskins, but at this altitude they were glad of the warmth that came from closeness and the smouldering ashes of the fire.

The dog curled up on the remaining floor-space, adding both to the warmth and to the pungent odour of the sheepskins. "Sleep well!" said Andrea. "Nobody walks the hills at night. And Pepito would warn us."

He lay down and seemed almost at once to be asleep. Rick listened for a few minutes to his measured breathing, then himself drifted into unconsciousness.

When he woke it was daylight. Andrea was crouched over the reviving fire. There was no sign of the others, but soon Blair came in, flicking Rick cheerfully with a damp towel. He looked pink and fresh, his bald forehead gleaming, his receding hair dark with moisture.

"Can't get used to not shaving," he grumbled.

"Andrea's boiling water for coffee, sir – he could spare you a mugful for a shave..."

"No, thanks. No sense in disguising yourself and then giving the whole show away – the 'officer-and-a-gentleman' touch. But I hate feeling scruffy." Blair rubbed his stubble with disgust.

Rick was glad to skip a daily chore which for him was hardly necessary yet, but had been unavoidable at his training camp.

"Did Charlie get an answer last night, sir?"

"Yes. Good reception too. 'Keep in touch,' they told us, 'good show.' Not much more they could say until we've something more definite to report."

"We're in contact, anyhow," said Rick with feeling. "That's a relief."

He went down to the icy little rivulet and stripped to the waist. Charlie was towelling himself vigorously in the pale early sunshine. All at once Pepito raised his head, barked sharply, and raced away down the slope, plumed tail streaming behind.

Charlie and Rick were instantly alert. "What's got into him?" said the Welshman.

"Someone coming, obviously —"

"But who? This early?"

"Best get back to the hut."

Their pistols were inside. On the journey they had been hidden with the equally tell-tale map in Charlie's case. Now they would normally carry them at all times. Rick cursed his own carelessness. On this very first occasion he had broken a simple rule: if you *have* a gun, don't leave it lying around. No matter how safe you feel.

And he *had* felt safe up here with Andrea. Andrea had said he never saw a stranger for weeks on end. Yesterday had been so deceptively peaceful. Yet some suspicious eye must have marked their passing, someone reported it. If the Carabinieri had been told they would not be so easily dealt with as the policeman in the piazza. No panic, he told himself. Mustn't run for the hut. Walk normally. Pray that they'd reach it before anyone spotted them.

He glanced back. The dog had vanished below the crest. His bark was muted by distance. But now a human head and shoulders rose to view, silhouetted against the morning brilliance.

"Only one man, by the look of it," he gasped, thankfully.

"Not even one man, boy-o!" Charlie's laugh was always faintly musical. "Even at this range I reckon I can tell when a girl is a girl."

EIGHT

The newcomer came into full view, her long dark hair swinging across her shoulders as she turned left and right to Pepito, who was frisking round her in hysterical welcome.

Suddenly she saw Rick and Charlie. She stopped in her tracks, gripping her basket with both hands, as though about to wheel and run.

Andrea's voice rang out from the hut. "Lina! Do not be afraid, my little one. These men are my friends."

He strode down to meet her. The two young men stood back, grinning amiably as they struggled into their shirts. Andrea and the girl embraced warmly.

"My granddaughter, Rosalina," he explained. "She comes every Saturday. Now I can offer you a better breakfast. She has brought up my fresh supplies." Blair came down from the hut to join them.

"I thought you were Germans," she said apologetically.

Blair snorted. "Why should you think that?"

"Not you, signore. Your friends." She giggled. "They were so *white*."

Andrea said sternly, but with amusement in his eyes, "Do you not recall the signorino Ricardo? The son of the learned Englishman, the *dottore* Weston, who used to dig up the Roman ruins in the Castle gardens?"

"Of course, grandfather!" She thrust out her hand and Rick clasped it. He remembered what the Italians were like with their constant handshaking. He smiled down at her. "You won't remember me," she said, challenging him.

"I'm sure I do," he lied.

Her eyes were mischievous as they saw through him.

Yet how could he be expected to remember her? She was — what? Fifteen? Perhaps younger. Italian girls seemed to grow up so quickly. When he was last here, a lordly fourteen-year-old, she must have been about eleven, one of a crowd of schoolgirls in smocks, racing out of the schoolyard with their briefcases. He, the foreign boy staying at the inn, was known by sight to everyone. It meant nothing that she remembered him, of course she would. Or that he did not remember her — of course he wouldn't.

They walked up to the hut together. "It's a long climb from the town," he said, "you must be tired."

"Oh, no." She tossed her head. "I have not come all the way from the town. Our farm is half-way up the valley. Down there." She gestured. "Five kilometres only."

She was barefoot. She moved lightly and confidently. Dropping behind her as they reached the doorway, Rick noticed what good legs she had. So did Charlie. Nor did Charlie miss Rick's look. He winked. "We must remember the rules – *sir*," he murmured with mock respect.

Rick did not need the reminder. It had been impressed upon him during his weeks of intensive training. Agents would meet all kinds of temptation. They must never become emotionally entangled, but concentrate ruthlessly on the job in hand.

Andrea and his granddaughter exchanged family news while she unpacked the basket and made coffee for them all. The others sat outside. She came out and filled their mugs. The shepherd followed, offering thick slices of crusty bread, thinner slices of ham and wedges of cheese.

"We are eating you out of house and home," Blair protested.

"I will come again in a day or two," said Lina. "I can bring extra."

"But then —"

"Have no fear," said Andrea. "I know what you are thinking, major. If she brings extra food, questions may be asked. Who is sharing grandfather's provisions?"

"Exactly."

"Do not worry. My Lina is most discreet. Certainly, questions will be asked. But it will be all in the family."

Rick pondered the phrase, "all in the family", as he sipped the steaming coffee. He knew how much the family counted in Italy. In a sense this family was already involved in spite of itself, committed by

Andrea's decision to shelter the British parachutists. No one could now betray them to the authorities without also betraying Andrea. And what Italian would inform against his own grandfather?

Lina herself was obviously sympathetic. She sat back against the wall, black skirt drawn demurely over golden legs, stroking the fortunate Pepito with one hand and clutching her mug with the other. Her eyes roved from face to face as they talked.

"Anything," she exclaimed, "that will give us an end to this terrible war!" Everybody was now saying the same, she declared. Well, *nearly* everybody. Most of those who were not were thinking it, but were too frightened of the Fascists to speak their minds.

Blair spoke quietly, but confidently, of the coming Allied victory. In these past few weeks the Americans and British had occupied the whole island of Sicily. Sicily, as the map showed, was only a giant stepping-stone to the Italian mainland. Very soon now the Allies would make their next leap. They would push the Nazi armies back into their own Germany. The Italians would be free to drop out of the war.

"You cannot come too soon!" cried Lina vehemently.

Rick remembered what Andrea had said last night, about one of his grandsons dying on the Russian front. Perhaps he had been Lina's brother?

But, Blair continued gently, the Italian people must help themselves. There were ways of hastening the end of the war. In France people did all they could to harass the Germans who had overrun their country. In Yugoslavia, where it was wild and mountainous, there were guerrillas fighting heroically.

"Do you think that Italians would do such a thing,

signorina?" His cool grey eyes were fixed upon her.

"I – I think they might," she said uneasily, "but you understand, signore, it is difficult for us."

"Of course. And it takes great courage. But a whisper has reached us, even in London, that things are beginning to move. Perhaps even in this region."

She hesitated. "One hears things, yes. But one does not know how much to believe."

Blair lit a cigarette slowly and deliberately, giving her time to think. "I have come – with Ricardo and Charlie – to find out. I wondered if you could help us?"

Again she hesitated. Then she looked up at him. "I have heard – there is a little band of men – in the hills . . ."

"Yes?"

"I cannot tell you where. They move on, constantly."

"Naturally. But somehow we have to establish contact."

She nodded. Then, taking the plunge, she said, "You might try Giovanni Lamberti, at the inn . . ."

"The Tre Corone," said Rick, "where my father and I used to stay. If anyone knows what is going on in the district, Lamberti will."

"Innkeepers usually do," said the Scot drily. "But – is he dependable?"

Rick looked at Lina. "I would swear it," she said.

"Why are you so sure?" Blair demanded.

"I help them out, down there, on Saturday and Sunday nights when they are busy. I serve, I wash dishes. It is so lonely up at our farm. I like to see a little of the world."

Good for you, thought Rick. This girl was not born just to milk goats and rake the hay.

"You have some notion of his political views?" Blair was probing gently.

"He's no Fascist, that's for sure! He has no use for Mussolini. Naturally, he must guard his tongue – be agreeable to all his customers."

"All the better. We don't want a chatterbox."

"He was never that," said Rick.

Lina asked if she should speak to Lamberti, sound him out. Or would the signori come down to the Tre Corone tonight, when she would be working there, and she could vouch for them?

Blair seemed reluctant to commit himself. Say nothing yet. Perhaps tomorrow. Perhaps in a few days. There were many things to consider...

Rick felt sorry for the girl. She was so obviously eager to help. Blair was almost snubbing her. It was puzzling, for he knew Blair's anxiety to get to work without delay.

So Lina picked up her empty basket with nothing settled. "All right if I see her on her way?" Rick murmured. Blair nodded.

"By all means."

"It'll refresh my memory – the lie of the land..."

"Of course." Blair looked faintly amused but was, thought Rick, surprisingly co-operative.

Rick needed no refreshing of his memory about the way down into the valley that led eventually to Sant' Arpino. It followed the stream which, after a few hundred yards, plunged into the green gloom of the woods.

It was a pleasant change, though, to be walking with a girl after spending the last six months almost entirely in all-male company. They talked of his pre-war visits, and of his dead mother. "So, Ricardo, you must have also Italian relatives?"

"Yes. But of course we've lost touch since the war. And mother was an only child, so I haven't any uncles or aunts or cousins on her side. I think my grandfather is still alive – in the North, though, in Padua – but we've had no word since 1940."

"It is sad! But I see now why I can talk to you so easily. I was a little afraid of your major. He is very... severe."

"Oh, he doesn't mean to be." He sang Blair's praises, from what little he had learnt – and guessed – of the Scotsman's war record.

They walked on. Further than he had meant to. But he had not noticed time or distance. It was Lina who stopped suddenly. "I think you should turn back now, Ricardo. We might meet someone. It would be only my father, most likely, but there would have to be explanations. And I have promised to tell no one." She put out her hand and he clasped it solemnly. They went their ways. He was glad that he turned to wave for she, too, was looking back.

He found Blair sitting on the shady side of the hut, smoking thoughtfully. He apologized for being absent so long. "But I've checked up on the path down to the town. I could find it now in the dark if necessary."

"Just as well. We'll be going down there tonight."

"*Tonight?* But you told Lina..."

"I know I did. But remember the rule: never advertise your movements in advance unless you have to. When we show ourselves in Sant'Arpino we're putting our heads in the lion's mouth. We have to. But we don't have to tell the lion when to expect us."

"You don't trust the girl?"

"Oh, I think she's straight enough. But she might let

something slip by accident. And once the inquiries start – well, some of these swine have tricks to bend the straightest of us. I've seen things in France." Blair's tone was grim. "It's a rough game we're playing."

Tonight the two of them would walk down to Sant' Arpino, mingle with the Saturday evening crowd and watch for a chance to make contact with the innkeeper. Charlie must stay at his post beside the radio transmitter.

Having made friends with the dog, the Welshman had now established an amicable – though almost wordless – relationship with his master. "It's the sheep," Charlie explained. "He can see I know something about them. Should do! My grandad has a little farm, Abergavenny way."

Andrea was shearing his sheep, working his way round the flock by degrees. There was nothing here like the sociable mass shearings Charlie had known at home, when all the neighbours helped each other out. When Andrea had a load of fleeces ready, Lina's father would bring up a donkey to collect them. Rick interpreted this for Charlie. Once Charlie had shown himself handy with the clippers, Andrea was glad to let him take a turn.

"Good thing," said Blair. "All makes for goodwill. And boredom is one of the snags about our job."

Rick could see that. He was thankful when, towards sunset, Blair said, "Right. Let's be on our way."

At a moment less fraught with danger it would have been a pleasant evening walk down through the woods. As it was, the dense ranks of the oaks and chestnuts walled them in, left and right, with a suggestion of prison bars, and there seemed something oppressive in the canopy of foliage overhead, cutting out the last brightness of the day. Rick pointed to a fainter path, forking off and ribboning away to the other side of the valley. "I think that leads up to the Scarlatti farm. Lina said she lived at the back of beyond. I can believe it!"

They came down into the open valley, suffused by the golden glow of sunset. Sant'Arpino huddled below them, all beige walls and rusty pink tiles, the dome of the church sitting like a hat on the centre of the town. Rick identified the other landmarks. The Convent nestling for protection close to the Castle, with its oddly-shaped swallow-tailed battlements perched on its tawny precipice...

"The excavations are over there to the right, sir, in the gardens. I expect they've been covered over for the duration."

"Expect so." Blair had no interest in Roman villas.

"I was always a bit scared of the Conte – he was rather grand. I liked the Contessa. She was awfully nice to us. I wonder if they're in residence – they have a villa in Rome and a palazzo in Venice —"

"You'll not have much chance to pay a social call."

"*Me?* The Contessa? Good lord, sir..." As a boy, he had admired her from afar, but even in peacetime the idea of calling on her would never have occurred to him.

The murmur of the town swelled as they drew nearer into the hubbub of a Saturday evening. There had been so much life on those bygone Saturday evenings. In summer the people of Sant'Arpino, like most Italians, preferred to live in the streets, especially the piazza, parading up and down, all the girls together, all the young men together – at least to begin with. Even the old folk took chairs and sat in their doorways or called and gossiped incessantly from upstairs windows

66

and balconies.

Things hadn't changed much. True, there were no longer the garish lights strung from tree to tree across the piazza — there must be some sort of black-out regulations. But music still blared from the amplifiers even though it was now more military marches than dance tunes. And once it was interrupted by a bulletin of war news to which nobody seemed to listen.

The laughter and chatter went on unchecked, the self-conscious hip-swinging parade... Only it was noticeable that the girls far outnumbered the young men and some of the young men were in no condition to strut to and fro as in the old days. Many limped or greeted their friends with a left handshake, dangling an empty right sleeve. The war had not missed Sant' Arpino.

This reminder of the war recalled Blair's earlier remark: when they showed themselves in Sant'Arpino they'd be putting their heads in the lion's mouth. He mustn't forget. This wasn't the friendly town he had known as a carefree boy. Behind all this gaiety, it was full of lurking dangers.

The square, as usual in Italy, was dominated by a rugged statue of Garibaldi, the national hero of the nineteenth century. As they neared it Rick murmured, "There's Lina!"

She was seated on the plinth of the monument, slipping on the high-heeled shoes she had been carrying. He would have known her anywhere, though she had done her hair, changed her dress and generally smartened herself up for the evening. But that small neat figure, the resolute chin, the Roman nose, were unmistakable. On an impulse he said softly, "*Buona sera!*"

She was on her feet instantly, head tossed haughtily

to face him. He was more certain than ever that he had made no mistake. The almond-shaped eyes were Lina's too, though they showed no sign of recognition.

"What do you take me for?" she demanded.

He was so taken aback that caution for a moment deserted him. "I... I'm sorry. But surely, after this morning..." He made another misjudgement. He took a step towards her, hands spread in a gesture of apology.

"This morning?" Her tone was withering. "I have never seen you in my life before." She turned abruptly and marched away through the crowd. There was indignation in the very click of her heels on the paving. Rick flushed. People were staring.

"That wasn't very clever," said Blair mildly.

"But it *was* Lina!"

"Of course it was. But you didn't have to speak to her just then. And stupid to persist when she obviously had her own good reasons for pretending she didn't know you. This place is a bit public. Full of people who know *her*."

"I *am* a clot," said Rick miserably.

Blair did not contradict him. "Let's have a coffee. Give her time to start work at the inn. And when we do get there, take your cue from her. Let her speak first."

"You do think it's all right, sir?"

"Yes. It was too risky here. The lassie's hard-headed, for all her pretty face."

Rick recovered his composure as they sat under the café awning. Through the trees he could see the white frontage of the Tre Corone with its balconies and shutters. In a few minutes he would be meeting good old Lamberti. Everything would be all right.

The tables were crowded with local regulars. New people constantly arrived, saluting friends with handshakes and laughter and kisses. Suddenly he became aware of figures hovering in the shadows, as though waiting for their table when it became vacant. Blair, though his back was turned to them, was conscious of their presence, for he turned and remarked pleasantly over his shoulder, "We are just leaving, signori, this table is at your disposal..."

One of the men stepped forward. Rick saw the uniform of the Carabinieri, the spotless white sword-belt slanting across the chest. A curt voice spoke.

"You are *not* leaving, signore. It is not your table we require but yourself and your friend. You will be good enough to come with us to the station."

NINE

The Carabinieri headquarters were just off the square.

In the poster-hung outer office they met the suspicious scrutiny of the duty-sergeant.

"Your papers, signori!"

Blair slapped down his identity card. Rick did the same but in a more respectful manner. His heart was racing. He struggled to maintain an outward calm.

The sergeant examined the cards and looked satisfied.

So he should be, thought Rick much relieved. Any forged documents issued to SOE agents were the work of professionals. Scotland Yard recommended the best men they knew. Forgers, like burglars, safe-blowers and other crooks, were quite patriotic and delighted to put their skills at the disposal of their country. Especially if they happened to be in prison at the time and could earn extra privileges or remission.

"And what brings you to Sant'Arpino, signore?"

"A family matter," said Blair with dignity.

"And you..." The sergeant glanced at Rick's card. "A family matter also, Signor Calvino?"

"Yes, sergeant." Keeping up his diffident manner Rick started on the cover story he had so often rehearsed in readiness for such an occasion.

He had been born in these parts but, while he was still a baby, the family had moved south to Bari. This year their home had been destroyed in an air raid. (A safe story, this, for the port of Bari was a favourite target of the British and Americans.) Ricardo was heading back to his native region to seek help from an aunt.

"And her name?" The sergeant waited, pen poised.

"Unfortunately," said Rick, "there was a little difficulty here." His aunt had lost her husband in the North African campaign. She had just married again and somehow – the family not being great letter-writers – he wasn't sure of her new name or where she now lived. But he could find her, he *would* find her, he had vowed to his dying mother, God rest her soul...

"Yes, yes. So – you are not with this signore?"

"Only since this morning," interrupted Blair. "He asked me for a lift."

"Ah, Signor Morelli, I was coming to that. You have a car?"

"I *had* a car." Blair swore with a fluency that impressed Rick. You did not learn words like that from phrase books. "Now," concluded the major running out of bad language, "I fear it is a total loss."

"And where is it, signore?"

"God knows! The accident happened miles from

71

anywhere. This young man helped me to push it out of sight in a wood. No one could drive off with it, but there was my baggage. Which explains why, after tramping endless kilometres, I arrive in your town with nothing but the clothes I stand up in."

"In the morning we will find your car."

You won't, you know, thought Rick uncomfortably. And that would mean trouble. But with luck they would be back in their hiding-place at Andrea's hut. Blair's answers, like his own, seemed to be going down all right. They might soon be free to leave.

In the first few minutes he had been properly scared. Had the charming Lina been deceiving them that morning? Had she really turned them over to the Carabinieri? Incredible, yet – the hard-boiled Blair would say – not impossible. But if the Carabinieri already knew that they were British, why this low-key routine questioning? He was feeling more cheerful now. Lina's odd behaviour in the piazza had been due to caution. Nothing to do with the Carabinieri. They, after all, had a duty to watch out for suspicious strangers.

"Would you please turn out your pockets, signori?"

"This is ridiculous," said Blair. "I am a respectable businessman. Just because I crashed my car on your infernal roads do you suppose that I am a criminal?"

"I suppose nothing. It is a regulation." The sergeant spread out his hands in an apologetic gesture. He was clearly afraid of complaints to higher authority afterwards.

"Very well – but be quick about it. I have still to find somewhere to sleep tonight."

They emptied their pockets along the counter. Rick watched, heart in mouth.

The sergeant snapped open Blair's cigarette case.

72

Luckily it was the real one, with a row of cigarettes that brought a wistful exclamation from the sergeant – and an invitation from the major to help himself. He was not carrying the fake, a flat metal box purporting to hold fifty cigarettes but actually containing his miniature radio receiver with its tiny earphones and 80-volt long-life battery.

The sergeant barely glanced at Blair's cigarette holder. It looked so completely ordinary, even to the nicotine stains, although actually it embodied a tiny telescope only an inch and a half long.

Blair's impressive row of fountain pens was normal enough for a businessman. But one, Rick knew, was designed in two parts. The first held the ink supply, the second a small but effective dose of tear gas which could be squirted in the face of an enemy.

Their handkerchiefs passed without comment, the invisible maps remained invisible. The large wad of currency notes in Blair's body-belt did not raise an eyebrow. For a businessman, perhaps engaged in some highly confidential deal, the cash meant no more than the smaller amount in the trouser pocket of a young nobody like Rick.

Even Blair's pistol was accepted as a sensible precaution. "There are some strange characters about these days," said the sergeant more truthfully than he realized. "And we Carabinieri cannot be everywhere."

There was more surprise when Rick's own weapon was produced. But Blair broke in smoothly, "This is mine, too. When the car broke down in that lonely spot I handed it to him – it was more sensible that we should both be armed..."

"Quite so, signore. In these troubled times there are army deserters as well as bandits."

"I am not so much concerned with bandits," said Blair grimly, "I am looking for the man who has stolen my wife."

This, thought Rick, was an inspired touch. A British bobby would have been instantly alert lest a "domestic dispute" developed into homicide. This sergeant reacted quite differently. How natural, if some scoundrel went off with your wife, that you should track him down and take your revenge! Honour demanded it. Strictly, of course, the police should stop you – if they could. But their hearts would not be in the job. Their sympathy would be all with the avenger.

Blair had prepared his story well. His business partner had swindled him and finally run away with his wife. The sergeant listened entranced. So did the half-dozen other Carabinieri gathered in the charge room.

There was a wealth of dramatic incident. Blair was (Rick knew) lumping together a number of real-life occurrences drawn from the scandalous gossip of the hotel lounges at trade fairs he had attended in peacetime at Turin or Milan. But he was also (Rick guessed) drawing upon misfortunes in his own private life. Blair had a daughter but never mentioned a wife. Or "home", which Rick suspected was very much a broken one. Whatever Blair's own past had been, he acted the part of the imaginary Alessandro Morelli with absolute conviction.

It was a good cover story. It explained a city man's presence in this remote countryside. It explained why he could not produce any local people to vouch for him – he was not on holiday, not visiting friends, not calling on customers. It was a romantic story with which any Italian husband could sympathize. If Signor

Morelli was behaving wildly, it was because he was under stress.

We are home and dry, thought Rick exultantly, studying the rapt faces of the Carabinieri. He almost believed in the story himself. The sergeant was clearly persuaded. Blair paused to offer cigarettes all round. He confessed that he was suddenly realizing how exhausted he was. And he had still to find a hotel...

"The Tre Corone is a modest establishment for a gentleman like yourself," said the sergeant, "but it is clean and comfortable."

At that moment there was a warning murmur from the man nearest to the door. "The Peacock is coming!" There was an immediate change of atmosphere. The sergeant stiffened. Cigarettes disappeared.

There was a brisk step outside. As the door opened everyone sprang to attention. The sergeant saluted.

The odd reference to "the Peacock" was instantly explained. The man who entered was arrayed in the peacetime splendour of a captain's full-dress uniform. A cockaded hat, a voluminous cloak, open to reveal a black swallow-tailed coat and black trousers with a broad red stripe, a dangling sword...

"Anything to report, sergeant? I am due at the Castle."

A formidable face, carefully shaven, with a thin moustache that might have been pencilled... A heavy perfume, prevailing even over the tobacco smoke and the sweat...

A human peacock indeed! Rick guessed he was wearing a corset. He knew that cavalry officers sometimes did, to produce a more youthful figure.

"I was questioning these two men, captain. Being

strangers in the town. They were observed in the piazza —"

"Quite right. We cannot be too careful at this time."

The sergeant cleared his throat nervously. "I did not think it necessary to trouble you —"

"I am here to be troubled, Villani. But not now – I cannot keep the Contessa waiting for her dinner. In the morning."

"I hardly think it is necessary, captain."

"I am the one who must decide what is necessary," said the officer grandly. "I had better talk to these men myself. We cannot afford to make mistakes. Detain them overnight."

Rick's heart sank.

"Of course, captain," said the sergeant.

"I shall be at the Castle. But do not call me out unless the matter is vital."

"Of course not, captain!"

Still, despite his important dinner-date, the officer lingered, eyeing the two suspects in a manner that Rick did not altogether like. The sergeant waited, deferential. The captain said, thoughtfully, "Lock them in the cell at the end of the passage."

The sergeant looked surprised. "But, captain – you will remember that —"

"I remember everything. Be good enough to do as I say."

"Of course, captain. The cell at the end of the passage."

The Peacock was gone, the sergeant obsequiously at his heels. Only the perfume remained, hanging on the stuffy air. A car door banged in the street. The sergeant returned and took down a key.

"I greatly regret this, signore. It is the war. Captain

Collodi is very strict. You understand, I have to obey orders."

"I suppose so." Blair put out a casual hand to pick up his cigarette case.

"Forgive me, I must keep everything until tomorrow. It is the regulation." The sergeant relented only sufficiently to extract two cigarettes and push them across together with Blair's matches. Then, with two Carabinieri at their heels, he led them down a corridor and unlocked a door with iron bars across its upper section.

The detention, he repeated, was just a regrettable formality.

But it was a detention none the less, thought Rick with suppressed fury. With an officer like Captain Collodi, Sergeant Villani was taking no chances.

TEN

"Nothing so subtle as a peep-hole," Blair whispered with approval. It was safe to use English. Thanks to the barred top of the door they had a clear view down the corridor and could make sure that nobody was listening.

It was their only consolation. The situation had taken a nasty turn.

They faced more questioning in the morning and the captain might be harder to deceive. Blair's Italian was fluent enough for everyday contacts – but was it so faultless that no tiny slip would give him away? And supposing the Carabinieri did the obvious thing, drove them back along the road they claimed to have come by, seeking the abandoned car to back up their story?

Rick thought wistfully of their guns, now confiscated along with Blair's tear gas fountain pen. Should they have let themselves be so tamely arrested? Or fought their way out at the beginning?

Common sense told him that to fight would have been folly. When *could* they have escaped? At the café table in the piazza? In the guard room when the sergeant was questioning them – with half a dozen armed men within call? Their chances of getting clean away would have been slight. And the mere attempt to do so would have shown that they had something to hide.

No, Blair had been right in trying to bluff it out. He had nearly succeeded. Only the captain's arrival had thrown a spanner in the works. Now they must think again.

Rick watched the corridor through the door bars while the major prowled round the cell. It was a very ordinary cell. Two beds made of hard planks and fixed to the walls, folded army blankets, a bucket. One small barred window, high up, but not too high for a glimpse of the outside world if a tall man stretched.

"Someone coming," said Rick softly. He lapsed back into Italian to be on the safe side.

Something smelt good, which made a welcome change in this place! He stood aside as the key turned and a man entered with a cloth-covered tray. The sergeant poked his head in. Another man hovered behind him.

"As you have not been charged yet, signori, you are allowed to have meals brought in. At your own expense, naturally."

"Naturally!" said Blair sourly.

"I ordered this from the hotel."

"You have shown admirable initiative, sergeant."

Blair was maintaining his pose of innocent indignation. He accepted the hot veal, the peaches, the cheese, the carafe of red wine, as of right. He demanded the *gabinetto*, disdaining the sergeant's indication of the bucket in the corner. In turn he and Rick were escorted to a lavatory.

When they were alone again, the meal over and the tray removed, the major lit one of his precious cigarettes.

"I fancy our sergeant is a rather nervous man. He wants to avoid trouble if I do prove to be a highly respectable person. At the same time he's equally scared of this – Captain Collodi, isn't it?"

"I think that was the name, sir."

"I suppose we shall become better acquainted with *him* in the morning. Though I'd rather not."

At this point the light went out. Bedtime, presumably, for prisoners. From the passage a pale band of light still streamed through the bars in the door.

Rick crossed to the window and stood on tiptoe. The night air brought the healthy tang of the stables. He could hear horses shifting and stamping. Gripping the bars, he hoisted himself up for a clearer view.

To the right lay the archway through which, years ago, he had watched the patrols ride out on their duties. The moonlight fell on the tall wooden gates folded back on their hinges. Were they shut, he wondered, later on?

One of the bars shifted in his grip. He dropped lightly to the floor.

"It looks over the yard," he reported in a whisper. "And the gates are open to the street."

"Fine! When our friends have settled down for the night we'll see what we can do with our little saws. At least they didn't rob us of *them*."

"We may not need them, sir. The bars feel loose."

Blair tested them and chuckled. "Typical! These Italians are splendid workers – they can build anything. But they lose interest when it comes to maintenance."

"I doubt if the cells are ever used much. Perhaps an occasional drunk-and-disorderly. And *he'd* be too drunk to try climbing out through windows!"

It would certainly be much better if they could avoid using the surgical saws. It would make them far more suspect than before and the hunt would be on in earnest.

But anyone – even an innocent man – might take advantage of loose bars set in a crumbling window-ledge. There would be nothing to suggest anything sensational – least of all any wild notion of British agents.

An hour passed. The blaring music in the piazza was switched off. The horses ceased to snort and fidget. No voices or footsteps came from the yard.

"On our way," Blair grunted. "The first few minutes will be the trickiest. Getting clear of the town. But if we *are* stopped, no playing about – we run. We run like hell. And if we *can't* run..." He paused. "Then we must kill. Quietly. As we've been taught."

The bars gave no trouble. Rick laid them noiselessly on the floor.

"Better take them," said Blair. "Might be handy."

Rick slipped a bar into his trouser pocket, where it hung cold and heavy against his thigh.

"You first, laddie," Blair ordered. "Just in case I get stuck!"

It was almost a challenge to a contortionist, hoisting oneself up to the window-ledge, folding oneself into the opening and turning so as to drop feet first into the yard below.

There were a few anxious, agonizing moments. Rick squeezed and squirmed, belly pressed painfully against the unyielding edge of the stonework... Then he was through, dangling in the cool darkness, boots scrabbling against the wall outside... He let go, landed with catlike softness, and stood trembling.

Looking up, he saw the major's face, a pale oval in the moonlight. He was working his lean body into the twisted position that would enable him to get his legs through. For his age, thought Rick admiringly, he was a remarkably fit man. In a few seconds he'd be out, standing beside Rick and they'd be well on their way to freedom.

But Blair's wriggling was destined to be a waste of effort. A triumphant voice spoke from the shadows of the archway.

"That will do, signori! Do not move! Or we shall be compelled to shoot."

ELEVEN

Sergeant Villani stepped out into the moonlight, followed by three other men. Their carbines were levelled at Rick.

No hope of doing as Blair had ordered. How could you "run like hell" when four Carabinieri blocked the archway?

Blair was still trapped in the cell. He had vanished from the window. A noisy struggle was raging inside.

"Hands on the top of your head," barked the sergeant, "and keep them there!"

Rick could only obey. He was marched back into the building, but to a different cell. Soon a dishevelled Blair was hustled in to join him.

"Excellent!" said the sergeant. "Many thanks, signori, for acting so promptly – and in line with our expectations. You saved us a weary wait." His apologetic manner was gone. Smug triumph had replaced it. "We thought that the loose bars might tempt you. Now it's for you to convince us that you are law-abiding citizens. Not for us to prove we were justified in holding you."

So, thought Rick, we are properly in the cart.

Blair could no longer bluff these men by threatening to make trouble for them in high places. By attempting a break-out they had revealed a sense of guilt. Guilt of what? That was what the Carabinieri would now try to ferret out. It could only be a matter of time. Sooner or later their cover stories would crack under repeated questioning.

No chance of escape from this new cell. Its window bars were immovable. Their boots had been removed – together, had their captors only realized, with the saws concealed inside them.

Locked up again in the darkness Blair said, "Nothing to be done for the moment. Get some sleep – if we can."

Any discussion might have been dangerous. They could not be sure now that they would not be overheard. Silence was safest.

But, exhausted though he was, Rick could not get to sleep quickly. Too many anxieties made a turmoil in his brain. Eventually he dropped off and woke to grey daylight and a monotonous clanging of church bells.

"Sunday!" said Blair, sitting up with a yawn. "How about a nice lie-in with the papers? A walk with the dog? I *don't* think."

Thinking of those possible eavesdroppers Rick broke hurriedly into Italian.

"Very proper," said Blair, a little crossly. "But you

84

don't really imagine one of those chaps has been squatting outside the whole night, ears cocked to catch our first good morning?"

"Not really – signore. But..." Rick grinned. "I've so often had it impressed upon me that one can't be too careful."

"Fair enough." The major recovered his good humour.

It felt early. It might be hours, thought Rick, before the captain deigned to appear and take over the interrogation.

"Bet he had a late night at the Castle," he said wistfully. "Long luxurious dinner, best of wines, coffee in the loggia overlooking the gardens..." He checked his tongue. Mustn't voice his own memories. The Contessa had put on super dinner parties for the archaeologists. Young as he'd been, he had sometimes been included. He did not envy her the company she had had last night.

He thought of the pompous Collodi. Not the sort of guest the Contessa would have chosen. He remembered her as elegant and sophisticated, joking wittily with his father, her English almost perfect, only her pronunciation quaint. What must she think of the peacock captain? But under Fascism, even the nobility had to watch their step. He did not blame her for keeping in with the Carabinieri.

At last their door was unlocked. Mugs of grey coffee were set down sloppily on the floor, with hunks of dry bread. Then they were taken in turn to the wash place, an armed guard remaining watchful outside the open door. They heard more church bells, calling the townspeople to Mass. From a distant office a telephone rang from time to time.

"About us?" Rick suggested softly, eyebrows raised.

"Maybe. They're probably trying to check up on our papers and then the chaps at the other end will be ringing back. With results – if any!" Blair smiled, apparently his old confident self again. Rick wondered if it was just a mask to keep up morale.

It was an hour before the key turned again. "Morelli!" Blair was taken away, still managing to walk with a certain dignity without his boots. Rick settled down to await his own turn as calmly as he could.

He wondered what Charlie was thinking. And he wondered, rather miserably, what Lina Scarlatti was thinking. Did she know he was here? Had she anything to do with it? Where did she stand in this business?

Blair did not come back. But eventually the guard did. Rick, in turn, shuffled along the corridor and upstairs to the office where Captain Collodi, now in everyday uniform, sat frowning at the notes before him.

"Ah, the *young* man. Calvino?"

"Ricardo Calvino, captain."

"So I see here. Serving in what unit?"

It was said casually. Rick was ready for the trap. "No unit, captain. I am excused military service. A heart condition."

"All deserters say that! Have you a discharge paper?"

"The sergeant took it."

"Ah, yes. I see. I am sorry that you have got mixed up with this fellow Morelli. Tell me how you met him, everything you know about him. You have only to be open with us. Then the misunderstanding can be cleared up – so far as you are concerned – and you can go free."

86

"I know nothing about him, captain. I met him only yesterday morning. He gave me a lift." Rick kept to the agreed story that they had known each other only a few hours. Then there would be less risk of contradicting each other.

He stuck also to his story of the air raid that had wiped out his home and sent him in quest of a newly-married aunt whose name he did not know.

"You seem to be remarkably unlucky with air raids," the captain observed with deep sarcasm. "You appear to *attract* bombs."

"Captain?" Rick tried to look stupid.

"The address you give as your home was indeed damaged by the RAF two years ago. So was the record office where your birth was registered and also the one which issued your identity papers."

"Indeed, captain?" exclaimed Rick in amazement.

"Indeed, young fellow. We have checked. Sergeant Villani has been on the telephone most of the morning. His ear burns. Morelli seems to have a similar attraction for hostile aircraft. Not only the office from which *his* identity papers were issued, but the address he gives for his last business premises and also for his private apartment in Milan. In each case the local police tell us that the buildings have either been flattened completely or are so burnt out that it is impossible to check anything."

"Incredible!" said Rick politely.

"Something is incredible. But not the destruction – that is officially confirmed."

Collodi eyed him with a quizzical expression. Rick stood respectfully silent.

It looked as if the Baker Street boys had overdone it on this occasion. It was SOE practice, when preparing

87

forged documents, to use genuine addresses which no longer existed. They had plenty of information on air raid damage in enemy towns. It was often known in which cities the various public departments had been bombed. Private addresses were not so fully listed, but from one source or another London had compiled a useful number that would be hard to check quickly.

The captain mopped his face with a handkerchief. The scent was heavy in the hot room. "To get back to you," he said. "Can you establish your identity? Is there someone in Bari who would speak for you? Your last employer? Your parish priest?"

"Of course, captain."

Glibly he rattled off the details he had carefully memorized. Just as carefully Collodi wrote them down. Rick could only play for time. It was, after all, Sunday. Even if the police were unusually diligent, he told himself, they could hardly send back an answer before tomorrow or Tuesday. There hadn't been a murder or a bank robbery. It was a routine inquiry. They would surely take their time.

"Tell me," said Collodi, "if you are the respectable young man you claim to be, why did you climb through that window and try to make off, last night? Was that the action of a law-abiding citizen?"

"I *am* law-abiding, captain. But desperate – I have to find my aunt, I have to help my family! We have no home now, no money. We have been bombed by the British – why should I now be locked up by my own countrymen? Mother of God, what have I done to deserve it?"

"I wish I knew," said Collodi. "There is something odd about you."

He rose from his chair and prowled round the office.

"I am a soldier. I was in Africa. I have medals." He slapped his chest. "I should by now be promoted. But no, I am stuck in this one-horse town, a mere policeman, wasting my time on petty thieves and suspicious nobodies like you." He sank heavily into his chair again. "But Morelli might be a bigger fish! Something worthwhile." He suddenly banged the table. "Tell me something about Morelli!"

"I am sorry, captain. I have told you all I know."

"Then tell me again."

The old trick. Rick had been warned against it. They asked you the same questions over and over again. It wasn't that they'd forgotten what you'd answered the first time. They hoped that *you'd* forgotten, so that you'd contradict yourself, make some slip they could pounce on.

"This car, now. What make was it?"

Alarm bells rang in Rick's head. He and Blair had never rehearsed the story of the car crash – Blair had invented it on the spur of the moment. What make had Blair told them?

"I – I did not notice."

"You did not notice?" Collodi's tone was mocking. His shrewd eyes, black as olives, searched Rick's face. "I have never met a young man who was given a lift in an expensive car – *and did not notice the make*."

"My mind was on other things —"

"Naturally. Your aunt. Your newly-married aunt. Whose name also escapes you. And her present whereabouts. In this district everything seems to vanish." He counted on plump, pallid fingers: "Your aunt, the unfaithful Signora Morelli, Signor Morelli's scoundrelly, swindling partner, Signor Morelli's car..." He pressed a bell. Sergeant Villani came in.

"There is still no news of the car, captain."

"I want it found! If it exists. Meanwhile, take this young man's fingerprints. Tomorrow we can perhaps discover if either of them has a criminal record."

Rick was taken downstairs again. In the guard room his hand was seized, his fingertips inked, then pressed down on the white pad, turned roughly to left and to right, to leave clear prints.

The sergeant thrust out a pen. "Sign! Underneath."

In the nick of time he remembered to write *Ricardo Calvino*.

He was taken back to the cell. To his dismay there was no sign of the major. A tray was brought in with only one plateful of pasta. "Where is the signore?" he asked.

"That is no business of yours," said Villani.

He did not like the look of things. They were evidently going to be kept apart, the routine procedure for breaking down suspects and getting them to contradict each other. But why all this fuss? What could these people hope to pin on them?

Of one thing he felt sure: Lina, despite her unexpected behaviour in the square, had not denounced them. If she had wanted to give them away – if she had been stringing them along from the first – she would have told the Carabinieri all she knew. Collodi would have been well aware that they were British parachutists and would have conducted his interrogation on that basis. As it was, he clearly had no idea. His questions showed that he was groping in the dark.

Rick came to the conclusion that it was all a wretched accident. Some bored Carabinieri had tried to display their zeal by pouncing upon a couple of strangers. One thing had led to another and, with a self-important officer like Collodi, a trivial incident had been blown up into an elaborate investigation.

It would have been funny – if it had happened to someone else. But it hadn't. It had happened, by the very worst mischance, to Blair and himself. And if they didn't find their way out of the mess very soon it might have the most unpleasant consequences. This was not Britain, where the police could not hold you for long without bringing a definite charge. In an out-of-the-way place like Sant'Arpino they could probably keep you locked up for as long as they pleased.

He lay back on his hard bench, gloomily reviewing the situation. Things had gone far too well at the start – the parachute drop, the trek into the hills, the safe arrival and warm welcome at Andrea's hut. Then everything had gone wrong. The luck had turned against them. Now, at best, he and Blair looked like spending the rest of the war in captivity. At worst – and this was not just a possibility but an ugly probability – they'd be shot as spies.

Footsteps outside. The key turning. He looked up, hoping to see the major. But it was Villani again, with an armed guard. The captain wished to question him again.

Upstairs in his office, shutters tilted to keep out the afternoon glare, Collodi wasted no time.

"When did you first realize that this so-called Morelli was in fact an Englishman?"

The sudden question was shattering. Rick's thoughts raced – his mind went into a skid and only by a desperate effort did he regain control. "An *Englishman*?" he echoed faintly. Fortunately his flabbergasted reaction was equally in keeping with the part he had to play. "I had no idea, signore."

91

"You noticed nothing strange in his speech?"

"Nothing, signore. I – I thought it was the way they talk in the North."

"He comes from the North, all right," said the captain triumphantly. "But from a good deal further north than Milan. Of course, he speaks Italian remarkably well. I myself was at first deceived. I can well believe that you were. Whether a court would believe you is another matter. It is a very serious offence to help an escaping prisoner of war."

At those last words Rick's spirits rose a little. "A prisoner of war, signore?" He tried to sound shocked, incredulous.

"I feel sure of it. He has confessed nothing – as yet. But, mark my words, he is a British officer."

Collodi was no fool. That he could not tell the difference between a Scot and an Englishman did not matter in the least – even to Blair in his present predicament, though at other times he would have resented it.

What *did* matter, what might be literally the difference between life and death, was that Collodi had jumped to the conclusion that he was an escaped prisoner of war. Not a spy! Spies could be shot. Escaped prisoners were simply put back in the cage. It was their honourable duty to make the attempt. Both sides recognized that.

For a civilian to aid them was quite another thing. Rick's heart sank again. Unless he could satisfy the captain that he was a simple innocent, duped by a stranger, he would be in a far more dangerous position than Blair himself.

He spread his hands in a helpless gesture. "I am amazed, signore. If I had realized! But I suspected nothing."

Collodi surveyed him with a shrewd expression. "I will give you the benefit of the doubt – for the moment. You will assist us to the best of your ability —"

"Of course!"

"Tomorrow morning you will show us where this car was left."

"I will try, signore, but —"

"You are not suggesting that you lied about the car?"

"No, no, signore!"

Collodi smiled. "Then it will be very awkward for you, will it not, if you cannot find it? If it should prove, in the end, that no car existed?"

It would be more than awkward, thought Rick dejectedly, as he was taken back to his cell.

Evening came. From the piazza he heard the murmur of the town coming to life again. Amplified music throbbed through the cooling air. Marches, dance tunes, operatic favourites, the strident propaganda songs of the Fascist Party. Occasionally the music broke off for a public announcement or a news bulletin, but the voices were too distorted for him to catch more than a phrase or two.

A guard brought his supper. More pasta. A bowl of soup.

Rick asked if there was any special war news. The man said that fierce fighting continued in Sicily. "We are inflicting terrrible casualties on the British and the Yankees. Soon we shall be throwing them back into the sea." His poker face broke into a sour smile. "And if you believe that, young fellow, you will believe anything!"

Rick decided to risk a more personal question.

"What is happening to the signore who was with me? Morelli."

"You mean the British officer? He has been taken away. To headquarters. He must be interrogated at a higher level. To find out which camp he has escaped from. The sergeant thinks he was trying to reach Switzerland." The man rolled his eyes comically. "What a hope!"

He went. The cell grew darker. A feeble electric bulb came on. So Blair was no longer in the building, transferred somewhere else, probably many miles away. Rick was truly on his own now. A long, lonely evening to get through... And then the night... Yet, he thought wryly, why be in a hurry to get to tomorrow? It was hardly a day to look forward to.

The loudspeakers continued to pour out their metallic music in the distance. The Sunday evening crowds would be promenading up and down. Suddenly the music was cut off, an excited voice was booming out some public announcement. Normally it would have been received with little audible reaction and the insistent music would have been resumed. This time however there was a burst of cheering, which swelled to a deafening and continuous roar. People were chanting. It was like the thunderous impact of waves on the base of a cliff. He could distinguish nothing but the recurring sound doo-chay... DOO-chay...

He had heard it often enough in the old days – even in Sant'Arpino there had been Blackshirt parades and demonstrations. Well-drilled crowds had bellowed in unison, cheering Mussolini, their precious *Duce*... Only tonight no one seemed to be cheering him. There was a snarl in those excited voices. He strained his ears. It sounded as if their cry were "Down with the

Duce!" Could it be?

A whip cracked. Only – he realized – it wouldn't be a whip. It would take a gun shot to be heard against that din. Gun or whip, it cracked twice more. From the crowd burst a positive howl of anger.

Now the tumult in the piazza had overflowed into the street outside the building. There was no longer any doubt about the slogan they were chanting:

"DOWN – WITH – THE DUCE!"

There was shouting now inside the building itself. Heavy feet raced up the stairs and thundered overhead. Furniture crashed over, glass shattered. The clamour had reached the corridor outside his cell. A key groped, the lock clicked, the door swung back. Exultant faces filled the open doorway, yelling and laughing hysterically.

In the forefront, radiant, stood Lina Scarlatti.

TWELVE

There was a startling change in Lina's manner since the previous evening.

In her excitement she flung her arms round Rick and kissed him. "You are free! We are *all* free! Mussolini has fallen!" He cried out as her foot landed on his unprotected toes. "Sorry – but they took our boots..."

She glanced down, then turned and called shrilly to Sergeant Villani who was gibbering ineffectively in the background.

"Give the signore back his boots! And anything else you have taken off him!"

"But, signorina —"

"There's no 'but' about it. Tonight all Italy is free!"

The crowd in the corridor roared approval.

"Come," the girl said. She still held Rick's arm firmly. "Your friend is not here?" she whispered, as they followed the ebbing crowd back to the guard room, where there were even more people, some occupied in tearing down official posters and generally demonstrating their dislike of the Fascist regime.

"They say he has been taken out of the town – to some headquarters," he said.

"A pity! We could have freed him too. But your major will be all right – it will be the same everywhere, I am sure of it," she said confidently. "And *you* are safe, Ricardo!"

A burly workman was pulling down a huge framed portrait of Mussolini. He flung it on the floor and danced on it with solemn satisfaction, like a performing bear. The crowd applauded with delight. Two Carabinieri watched, doing nothing, their faces paper-white. Sergeant Villani came back with Rick's boots, which Rick donned thankfully and laced up.

"Let's get out of here," Rick muttered urgently.

But the girl was inexorable. "You have other items, sergeant."

"I have no authority, signorina —"

"But I am sure you have the signore's wallet, his pen perhaps, whatever was in his pockets?"

"I – I – I cannot possibly..."

She fixed him with her eye and he wilted visibly. "You see the mood of the people? They are very, very excited. Do you wish to see this building torn down about your ears?"

Villani protested no further. He unlocked a cupboard and set out Rick's possessions along the counter. After a moment's hesitation he even produced the pistol, which Rick thrust hastily into his pocket.

97

"If the signore would sign..." pleaded the sergeant, making a last effort to apply the regulations. Lina ignored him. "We will go now," she told Rick.

But Captain Collodi came rushing in from the street. His immaculate uniform was now crumpled and stained, he was bare-headed, his pistol holster gaped open and empty.

"What in God's name is going on here, sergeant?"

"We are celebrating!" cried Lina. And whatever Villani answered was lost in the chorus from the jubilant crowd: "*We are celebrating!*"

Collodi glanced round wildly. "This is a riot! I want this building cleared instantly. Instantly!" He saw Rick. "And this young man put back in his cell." Rick's hand flew to his pocket. But he had no need to draw his weapon. The huge workman who had been dancing on Mussolini's portrait turned now upon the captain, gripping him by the shoulders with his massive paws and shaking him.

"Tell us! Are you for the *Duce*? Or the King?"

Collodi began to bluster indignantly.

"The *Duce* – or the King?" the man insisted. "You have heard the radio? The little King has stood up to the bully at last. He has sacked Mussolini! Our precious *Duce* is under arrest. We have a new government. Now we may have peace. Can you wonder why we are celebrating? You had better celebrate with us. Or we may use this building as a bonfire!"

Collodi clutched at the tatters of his dignity. "Of course I am for the *King*. The Carabinieri hold their commissions from the King. Our loyalty —"

Rick did not wait to listen to his protestations. It seemed a good moment to go. He steered Lina deftly through the crowd and out into the night.

The darkness struck fresh and cool on his cheek. There was still plenty of noise. Bursts of singing, shouts, racing feet, cheers... Very different from an ordinary Sunday night in Sant'Arpino.

He hesitated on the corner of the piazza. An hour earlier, shown the open door to freedom, he would have made instinctively for the hills. But now, though he was still struggling to take in the new situation, he realized that everything had changed. He need not bolt like a rabbit for its hole. He might gain safety that way, but what else? Certainly not information, the information vital to his mission. What would Blair have done? Blair, he felt sure, would not have left the town without getting what he had come for.

Lina seemed to sense his momentary uncertainty. She pressed his arm. "We go to the Tre Corone?" she whispered. "You will be safe there. Tonight, you will be safe anywhere in the town."

They picked their way across the littered square. There was much broken glass, shreds of posters, a trampled Fascist flag, fragments of Party emblems torn down from public buildings... the axe heads and the rods, ancient symbols of power and punishment, now strewn in the gutter.

"Signor Lamberti looks forward to seeing you," she said.

"He knows?"

"He does now. I did as the major wished." She went on hurriedly, "I said nothing to anyone. But last night it was the talk of the inn – two unknown men had been arrested in the piazza. At once I thought of you. I had just seen you there." She gave an apologetic laugh. "I am sorry I had to pretend —"

"My fault. We were making for the inn."

"But you never arrived! So, when I heard about these strangers, I was very frightened for you. By this morning I felt sure it had been you and the major. So I told Signor Lamberti. I felt I *had* to do something."

"You were quite right. What did he say?"

"He was most sympathetic – he would see what could be done to help you. And this news tonight – it made everything much simpler. The town has gone mad."

"So it seems!"

They were threading their way with some difficulty towards the Tre Corone. There were still hundreds of people standing about in groups, some singing or chanting, others excitedly discussing the situation.

"What *has* happened, actually?" he asked her. "I haven't taken it in yet."

"I only know what was on the radio. Mussolini was outvoted at a meeting of the Fascist Grand Council. The King sent for him today and dismissed him. Then, it seems, he was put under arrest."

"Glory be!"

"I think that's what everyone in Italy is saying. The wireless speaks of demonstrations in all the cities – you can see how our own little town has taken it! People are saying it is the end of the war."

When they got to the Tre Corone the atmosphere was just as ecstatic inside. The wine was flowing. Someone was playing a guitar. The walls almost vibrated with chatter and song.

Their entry was unnoticed – except by the innkeeper himself, who enfolded Rick in a rib-crushing hug, kissed him on both cheeks and pushed him firmly down into a seat at a corner table. "Run to the kitchen, Lina!" he cried. "See what is left, even at this late hour.

100

The signorino must be famished."

Rick protested vainly. He would have preferred a less public place. "Is it all right?" he whispered cautiously. "No one must recognize me – Italy is still at war with Britain..."

"For a few hours longer – at most, a few days," said Lamberti airily, "while the formalities go through."

"Well, I don't want to be arrested again..."

"Have no fear!" Lamberti chuckled – coming from his vast barrel chest it was like a volcanic eruption. "The police have vanished from the streets. Even Collodi has made himself scarce! He drew his pistol when the crowd began tearing down the Fascist flags. That did it! It's a wonder he wasn't torn limb from limb."

"I saw him just afterwards," said Rick with a smile. "He *did* appear somewhat upset."

"Tell me," said Lamberti, "how is your eminent father? He is still spoken of here with great respect."

Rick answered as briefly as the innkeeper's torrent of questions permitted. He was trying to keep a clear head and concentrate his mind on immediate essentials. It was not easy, with the noise around him, the wine, the immense platter of meat and rice which Lina had just plonked before him, and the turmoil of his own emotions.

He clung to the thought of Blair. What would Blair have done at such a moment? Taken nothing on trust. That was for sure. Blair would have been sceptical about all these hysterical celebrations. Blair would have said, but the war *isn't* over and until we're sure it is we must act accordingly. Officially we are still the enemy. Once order is restored we may find ourselves back in the cells...

Our mission goes on, Blair would have insisted. Busi-

101

ness as usual until we get orders to the contrary...

But Blair wasn't here, unfortunately. Rick was on his own. And likely to remain so for the time being. He must try his best to do what Blair would have done.

That boiled down to two objectives: cut all this chatter – without offending the warm-hearted and admirable Lamberti – and obtain the hard information they'd come for. Then, tear himself away from the party and beat it through those dark woods to Andrea's hut on the mountain.

After a few minutes he managed to stem the flow and ask some questions himself.

"Yes," said Lamberti. "There has been some resistance already. But a mere handful of men until now. It takes courage, you understand —"

"Of course."

"But now, with Mussolini overthrown, people can show their true sympathies – as you see tonight..."

No time for fencing. Rick asked, directly, "Do you know who has been organizing the work so far?"

Lamberti hesitated only for a moment. "Yes, I know. To you, Ricardo, I feel that I can say it."

"Who, then?"

"He calls himself Pietro Rossi. It may not be his real name. He is a Communist, he is a life-long opponent of Mussolini. He fought against the Fascists in the Spanish Civil War – he is a veteran of the International Brigade —"

"The right kind of experience, I should think – for guerrilla war!" Now we are getting somewhere, thought Rick.

The innkeeper shrugged. "Of course, he is a Red – that is not to everyone's taste. Not everybody would respond to his lead. Perhaps that does not matter now?

With the end of the Fascists all people will come together – the Catholics, the Royalists, everyone who hungers for peace – they will demand a finish to the war..."

"We'll hope so. In the meantime how can I make contact with this Pietro Rossi?"

This time Lamberti's hesitation was lengthy. His eyes narrowed. "That is difficult, Ricardo. He... moves about. He is never in the same place."

Clearly, Rick told himself, even if Lamberti knows more, he is not going to divulge it. Most likely he's under some threat of fearful vengeance.

Well, as even Blair had once admitted, there were times when somebody just *had* to trust somebody else, or you got nowhere.

"Is there any way to send him a message?"

"Of course," said the innkeeper with obvious relief.

"Right. Tell him that a British military mission has been secretly established in the area..."

It seemed a rather grand description of himself and Charlie, but what else were they? And there was no room for false modesty. If he was going to get anywhere with this Rossi – persuade the man that he must be taken seriously – he would have to act the part.

"We are anxious to give him any help we can," he continued. "If a meeting could be arranged – a message can be sent back to me via Lina —"

"Will you not stay here, Ricardo? Your old room can be made ready in a few minutes —"

"Thank you, but I'm afraid it's impossible."

Terribly tempting, but of course utterly impossible. He was still in the lion's mouth. He must get out of here and back to Charlie... He needed the wireless anyhow...

"I am sorry." The innkeeper insisted on refilling his glass.

Suddenly Rick was conscious that a hush had fallen upon the crowded room. He heard a husky whisper.

"He has come."

All heads were turned expectantly towards the door.

The man who entered had one of the ugliest faces Rick had ever seen in his life. Only afterwards did he realize that it had not always been so. Probably it had always been rugged, but once it must also have been handsome. Now, with broken nose, a livid scar zigzagging across one cheek and the dent of an old wound disfiguring his temple, the man was a walking gargoyle.

Only – he walked like a king. Utterly confident. He came through the doorway and paused, surveying them all. Then he raised his clenched fist in salute.

"Good evening, comrades," he said quietly.

THIRTEEN

For a few minutes it was all exclamations and hand-shakes. The newcomer was lost to view as everyone crowded round him in welcome. Lamberti jumped up and went to join them. Rick alone kept his seat in the corner. He wished Blair were here. He was not sure how best to handle this sudden encounter. He would just have to play it by ear.

The newcomer's voice cut harshly through the babble. "Forgive me, comrades. Let us celebrate later. There's much to be done."

The crowd parted. He came striding across the room, the innkeeper at his side, motioning him towards Rick's table. He thrust out a hand. "I'm Rossi. Lamberti says you're British?" he murmured.

Rick stood up and shook hands. There was no point in concealment. "I am a British officer," he said in a similar low voice. "Lieutenant Weston."

"A lieutenant? You are very young." Rossi did not try to hide his disappointment.

"I am sorry. My superior officer is... not here." Did this man already know what had happened to Blair? For the moment Rick was giving nothing away unnecessarily. He remembered one of the major's favourite sayings, "information is often like food – it keeps better if it's not exposed to the air." Without giving Rossi a chance to ask where his superior officer *was* – and how Rick wished he knew! – he went on with all the dignity he could muster, "But in his absence I have authority to discuss matters with you."

True enough, he thought. In Blair's absence he had to carry on the mission as best he could. He was his own authority.

"It would be better to do that in private," said Rossi. "There are too many chatterboxes in here." He jerked his head scornfully towards the cluster of drinkers. "They think the world has changed in five minutes – just because that clown Mussolini has been knocked off his perch. Life is not so easy."

He beckoned Lamberti. The innkeeper nodded and ushered them into what Rick remembered as the family living room, full of ancient massive furniture and faded sepia family photographs. Rossi waved aside the offer of more wine and asked for water. "I prefer to keep my head clear." When Lamberti had gone, closing the door, he came straight to the point. "Now, lieutenant, what exactly are you doing here?"

"We were sent to make contact with any resistance movement that may be in this area."

"You have come to the right place."

"I hope so."

They faced each other across the table, keen-eyed, wary. Rick had, for the time being, forgotten the exhaustion of the past twenty-four hours. He was keyed up. This was not one of those polite conventional interviews. Resistance leaders were not like regular army officers. They were a tough breed of individuals, keeping to no rules. And Rossi was a Communist, with an inbred distrust of all governments except the Russian.

Blair had said, with heart-felt recollection of his French experiences, "We may find ourselves dealing with Communists. Splendid blokes some of them – but they can be tricky to handle. See everything in life from a completely different viewpoint. But we'd have to work with them, and thank God that they're on our side – for the moment, anyway."

"And what do you hope to accomplish?" Rossi enquired.

Rick decided to speak frankly. "Winston Churchill himself has set up a special organization..."

"Churchill? A fine man." Rossi's enthusiastic reaction was encouraging.

"He has defined our objective. It is, in his words, 'to set Europe ablaze'. We work with resistance groups in all territories occupied by the enemy. We are to cause maximum damage to Hitler and his allies – by sabotage, by armed struggle where appropriate, by underground activity of every type. To hamper their war effort in every way possible."

"Excellent!"

"Of course, the fall of Mussolini produces an entirely new situation. It changes everything."

"It produces a new situation," Rossi agreed, "but it

does not change *everything*. It is an opportunity, no more."

"No more?"

Rossi hammered his clenched fist into his other hand to emphasize his words. "It has to be exploited. Our friends out there –" he jerked his head towards the continuing sound of celebrations – "are innocents. They think one has only to tear up one flag and wave another. They sing and shout as if the war were over. Not so. Italy has a new government, that is all. The King has appointed Marshal Badoglio – a soldier, who will talk of national honour, of the need to continue the war..."

"But *can* he?" Rick tried to sound wise and well informed.

"He can *talk*," said Rossi contemptuously. "But the people must act. It's not just a new government we need, it's a revolution."

"You're a Communist, aren't you?"

"Does that frighten you?" Rossi looked amused.

"Not in the least. The Russians are Communists but they are our allies. Beating Hitler is all that matters. Even here in Italy the main enemy is Hitler. Mussolini may be gone but —"

"That is what I meant, it does not change *everything*. Hitler will not allow the Americans and the British to take over Italy. Matters here may get more desperate, not less. Let me ask you a plain question, lieutenant: can your people send us arms?"

This was the question Rick had expected – and feared. He must be careful about making promises. Blair had horrific stories of optimistic agents who had promised the earth to the resistance groups – and then been let down by the people at home. But it was a

108

question that could not be dodged.

"Yes," he said. "That is what we are here for."

"By air, presumably? By parachute drop?"

"It's the only way, in this country, I should think. Until you can guarantee us a safe landing strip."

Rossi nodded. "And that, for the moment, I cannot. It must be in the hills, where we are not observed. And where we can melt away before anyone gets after us!"

"How have you managed for arms so far?"

"The best we could. A peasant may have a shotgun, an army deserter brings his rifle, there are pistols." Rossi chuckled, a cold-blooded sound. "We have a saying, lieutenant – if you have a knife you can always get a pistol, when you have a pistol you can perhaps get a machine-gun. So – we arm ourselves from our enemies. But if the British will send us proper supplies —"

"I will report to my superiors," said Rick cautiously. "They will ask for information. How many men you have in your group, where you would want the arms dropped..." He saw impatience in the battered face opposite. "It need not take long – we are in radio contact – but I must have the information before they'll do anything."

"And suppose your radio message is picked up by the wrong people? Suppose that all the information I give you goes straight to the enemy?"

"It will be coded —"

"Codes can be cracked!"

"But everyone uses codes in war," said Rick patiently. "One has to take a chance. You want the arms, we want to send them. But if I make the recommendation, I must be able to show that it's a serious proposition, that you've an effective force operating..."

It was like getting blood out of a stone. Rossi remained vague. Some of his vagueness was justifiable, Rick realized. The size of his group fluctuated. The area of operations varied. They moved about constantly. It was impossible to maintain a fixed headquarters. All that made sense. But surely Rossi could have given him something more definite to go on? It was this passion for secrecy, the habit of conspiracy, the distrust of anyone who was not, like himself, a dyed-in-the-wool Communist...

Rick glanced at his watch. "If I went now," he said, "I should just have time to include something in tonight's transmission."

That did the trick. Rossi was obviously keen to get things moving. He stopped fencing. He did not give away much, but he told Rick enough for his immediate purpose.

Rick wondered if Blair could have done much better. This man was a hard nut to crack. He stood up. "When I get a definite answer, how can I contact you?"

The gargoyle features became a mask again, inscrutable. "*I* will contact *you*, lieutenant. Wherever you are, I shall be able to find you. For tonight you will be safe with the shepherd. Afterwards, who knows?"

They shook hands and parted.

Lina had been waiting in the kitchen of the inn, where the last customers had now departed. It was long past her usual hour for finishing work. Although, she said, she was accustomed to the lonely walk back to the farm, it had occurred to her that Rick would be going in the same direction.

How much had happened since their meeting yesterday and their first walk together in the morning sun-

110

shine! After the stresses of the past twenty-four hours, and not least the responsibility of handling this initial encounter with Rossi, it was a relief to be trudging through the moonlit woods with her.

Lina's cheerful confidence was a welcome change from the Communist's grim realism. Rick had not the heart to destroy her optimism. Like most of the people in Sant'Arpino the girl seemed to imagine that the war was as good as over. The Fascists were finished. In a few days everything would be sorted out.

"Don't worry about your major," she said. "Wherever they have taken him he will be all right. Perhaps already he is free! Nobody wants to go on fighting the British."

"I hope you're right," said Rick.

Lina was already looking forward to the future, to the wonderful days of peace that lay ahead. Eagerly she questioned him about England. She wanted to learn English, which hadn't been a popular idea at her school. She dreamed of seeing London, Buckingham Palace, the King and Queen, the two young princesses...

"Perhaps if I learnt English I could get a job? You have Italian restaurants? I have heard, there is a quarter in London – it is called Soho, yes? I could be a waitress. I do not want to end my days in a quiet place like this."

Quiet it was, certainly, except for the frogs croaking in the stream. But it was beautiful and, remembering London as he had last seen it, he wondered if she would enjoy the exchange. But he was certainly not going to discourage her. It might be fun if Lina turned up one day in England...

Meanwhile, free from that cell, he was not complaining of this Italian night. Lina had stopped talking. They walked in companionable silence. There were fireflies darting in the gloom. Suddenly he paused, his hand on her arm. "Isn't that a nightingale?"

She listened. "Yes. These woods are full of nightingales."

They went on again. He peered at the luminous hands of his watch. He thought of Charlie's radio transmission. But it was all right. There was more time than he had admitted to Rossi. He would walk much faster when Lina turned off to her home.

Now it was her turn to press his arm. She whispered, "I think there is someone following us."

Instantly he was tense again. His free hand stole to his pocket, seeking the reassurance of his pistol.

"How do you know?" he breathed.

She laughed softly. "A girl knows. But it has never happened to me before, going home to the farm. Perhaps it is *you* who are being followed. Perhaps it is one of Rossi's men."

"Ah!"

"For your protection – to make sure that you get safely back to grandfather's hut."

"Or to make sure that I really go where I *told* Rossi I was going," he suggested sceptically. It would fit in with the Communist's general attitude: don't wholly trust even your allies, if they don't carry a Party card.

They came to the fork in the path where their ways diverged. "Anyhow," he murmured, "I'll stand here for a few minutes. Then, if it's somebody following *you*, you'll have a clear start and he won't catch up with you."

"Thank you, Ricardo."

"I have never thanked *you* – for getting me safely

out of that police cell."

"It was nothing. I saw a chance when the people began breaking into the building..."

"All the same..."

He thanked her in the only possible way. Then gently, but with obvious reluctance, she detached herself from his arms. "Take care of yourself, Ricardo!"

"You bet!"

She turned and ran up the path, a shadow merging into the other shadows. He stayed quite still. The patter of her bare feet faded. Was it imagination, or could he hear other movements closer, but stealthily approaching? Abruptly, these sounds stopped. He could hear only the nightingale again.

Five minutes... The girl would be well up the hillside by now, almost home... Time to be moving himself. Time to get back to Charlie... The sergeant must be worried sick.

He struck out on his own path, walking as fast as the steepness and the faint light allowed. Once he stumbled and almost fell. Idiot, he told himself sharply. A silly little thing like a twisted ankle would ruin everything. Too much depended on him now.

He stood for a moment, regaining his breath. It was then that he heard below him the unmistakable clink of boot on stone. So the unknown pursuer, whoever he was, was interested in himself, not Lina.

What was best to do? He had his pistol. Should he turn and try to confront his shadower? But the man would simply stop, as he had done before, invisible in the gloom. Perhaps, as the girl had suggested, he was a friendly bodyguard assigned to him by Rossi. If he was also, as Rick himself was inclined to believe, sent as a check upon his honesty, why worry? He had told Rossi the truth, and the shadower could only report that he had. It was unlikely that the man was hostile – Rick could remember one moment at least, when he was saying good night to Lina, when a would-be attacker could have taken him off guard. Certainly it could not be a policeman. The disorderly celebrations in the town had driven all the police indoors.

The forest was thinning. The moonlight grew brighter, the stars showed between the treetops. Now the open upland stretched silvery to the sky. From the hollow, just beyond the crest, Pepito gave a warning bark.

At the edge of the trees Rick halted and peered back. Useless, of course, impossible to see a lurking figure . . . On a sudden impulse he called softly, "Good night, comrade! And thank you for your company!"

There was a smothered laugh from the darkness. A voice answered, "Good night, Englishman! Sleep well."

Somehow the tone was reassuring. Surely an enemy would not have spoken at all? Or would have sounded more startled? No, he was almost certainly Rossi's man. Rossi's parting words came back: "Wherever you are, I shall be able to find you. For tonight you will be safe with the shepherd." It had sounded like a guarantee.

Trudging up the last few hundred yards to the hut he wondered whether the man would now turn back and report to Rossi or remain on watch at the edge of the forest. Either way, it was a comforting thought that he was now under some sort of protection from the Resistance leader. Rossi had impressed him as a singularly effective character.

A dark figure loomed up against the stars. It was Andrea, as he expected, with Pepito padding silently at

114

his heels.

"Thank God!" called Andrea. "I knew it would be you. But where is the major?"

Rick began to explain. As they neared the hut Charlie emerged from hiding among the rocks some distance away. "You've had me worried," said the Welshman. The news of Blair naturally filled him with dismay.

With an effort he became rather more cheerful as Rick told his story, sitting beside the still-warm ashes of Andrea's fire.

"The major'll be all right. Talk himself out of it, I shouldn't wonder – especially the way things are going now, with Musso gaoled himself."

"Meantime," said Rick hesitantly, "it seems to leave me in command." He could not keep a slightly apologetic tone out of his voice. Charlie was so much his elder, so infinitely more experienced. It seemed absurd that he must give Charlie the orders, make the decisions... But Charlie said, "Not a doubt of that, sir. I'm only the 'pianist'."

"I think we must get a report off tonight. I must tell them what's happened to the major. And how I've made contact with Rossi. And ask about the possibility of getting him some arms for his group."

"I think they'll be needed, sir." Charlie had been scouring the ether during the past few hours, picking up English-speaking news bulletins from every source. What he had heard confirmed Rossi's estimate of the situation. "This new Italian government – Marshal What's-it – says it's going to continue the war at Hitler's side. But both the BBC and the Yankee commentators seem to think they'll crack once we start invading the mainland. That's when the Resistance will come in handy."

It was almost time for Charlie's nightly radio transmission. Rick took pencil and paper, goading his tired brain to the composition of a suitable message. He reported his meeting with Rossi, gave a cautious assessment of the man, his powerful character and his political line, and added the meagre details he had extracted from Rossi about the size and equipment of his group. He put in a plea that favourable consideration should be given to providing them with arms.

How much attention, he wondered, would the high-ups in SOE pay to this recommendation?

The nub of the ciphered message lay in the give-away words he had to include at the end: *Tartan arrested identified as British officer present whereabouts unknown* STOP *Pending fresh instructions I am taking over* STOP *Newboy* STOP

FOURTEEN

The next few days were anxious ones.

Rick hoped against hope that the miracle would happen – that suddenly Blair would appear, dishevelled but indestructible, and take over where he had left off.

Charlie remained obstinately confident: the major would come out of this as he had come out of tight corners before. True, to judge from the broadcast news – and Rick could understand the Italian as well as the Allied bulletins – it seemed as though Italy would continue the war. Rossi had been right. The people's hope of instant peace had been short-lived.

The demonstrations had ceased. The authorities had restored order. It did not look as if Blair had escaped, as Rick had, during the first hours of confusion. If he had he would surely, after this lapse of time, have contrived to make his way back. "He could have been shot by now," said Rick grimly, "if they came to the conclusion that he was a spy."

"Not if they think he's only an escaped prisoner of war. Not supposed to shoot you for that. Though I don't say the Nazis wouldn't. Luckily it's only the Italians who've got him."

"But suppose they blow his cover story? Collodi began to. And he'll be up against more experienced interrogators at headquarters. Even he might break down after days of it..."

Charlie shook his head. "You're forgetting the international rules. A prisoner of war is only compelled to give his name, rank and number. Doesn't have to say anything else. So he doesn't need a cover."

It was a comforting thought. But Rick still had to face the fact – Blair might escape the firing squad but he would still be a captive. Somehow "Newboy" would have to carry on.

The nightly signals Charlie received from his SOE superiors were not much help. There was no mention of any other senior officer being sent out as Blair's replacement. At the same time there was no suggestion that no one would be. Rick bore this uncertainty with mixed feelings. Sometimes the responsibility worried him. At others he felt a kind of exultation that he was running his own show, if only for a spell and in a very small way.

There was, as yet, not much show to run. He had not heard anything more from Rossi. It would be unwise to venture into the town again – he would be spotted by the Carabinieri, who would probably be delighted to put him back in a cell. He had to depend

118

on Lina's occasional visits to the hut to hear the local news and get an idea of conditions in Sant'Arpino under the new government.

Those visits were more frequent now. There were three people to feed at the hut. As Lina explained, without batting an eye, she would rather make the trip more often than carry too heavy a basket.

Then, very early one morning, Rossi came.

He came out of the mist, a shadow leading a file of other shadows. Pepito gave tongue and then, at a word from Andrea, fell silent.

Rossi advanced alone. His men, about a dozen of them, halted at a little distance, throwing themselves down with every sign of weariness. One had an army rifle, two carried shotguns. They had been carrying heavy wooden boxes with rope handles. At a sharp order from Rossi they took them to a spot further from the hut and stacked them with elaborate care.

"One cannot be too careful," Rossi explained to Rick. "We have been visiting a quarry. A long walk – and the boxes made it seem longer. But the effort was necessary."

"Dynamite, I suppose?"

"We must use whatever we can get, wherever we can get it. Until more regular supplies can be arranged." He gave Rick a very straight look. "Dynamite is handy for bridges, railway tracks, suchlike things."

"But you can't fight with it."

"You'd be surprised, my friend. Sometimes in Spain the Fascists were shooting at us from strongly fortified buildings. Often we had no artillery, no tanks or armoured cars. But we had brave men, coal-miners from the Asturias, who had brought sticks of dynamite from their pits. I saw one belt himself round with dynamite, making himself a living bomb. He crept forward, he threw himself against the gate..."

Rick gasped.

"He was, of course, blown to pieces," said the Communist coldly. "But so was the gate. Twenty-seven Fascists we killed! That miner would have thought it well worthwhile. But such sacrifices are wasteful of good men. With the right equipment we can win without these heroic gestures. So – " again the straight look that Rick had been dreading – "how do your people answer our request for arms?"

Rick cleared his throat. Andrea gave him a moment by interrupting with a mug of hot coffee, which Rossi accepted with a murmured acknowledgement but without taking his eyes off Rick's face.

"I made my report, Comrade Rossi. It is under consideration."

"Consideration?"

"You know what these people are —"

"Bureaucrats!"

"The SOE are hardly bureaucrats," said Rick gently. "But they have many requests – they are working in half a dozen different countries. Their resources are not unlimited. And they depend on the co-operation of the Air Force, the Army —"

"They are refusing us arms?" Rossi's voice was quiet, but terrible in its intensity.

"No, no, certainly not! But they ask for more information about you before they commit themselves. Can I, for instance, tell them about this raid on the quarry to get explosives? And how you plan to use them?"

"I have several ideas," Rossi said warily.

"You need not tie yourself. Give me one definite

possibility I can put to them."

"Very well. There is a big prisoner of war camp, not seventy kilometres from here. Ponte San Cataldo. It is full of British and Australian soldiers taken in the desert war. Americans too, Poles, French, Greeks. There is a section for officers."

"Yes, Comrade Rossi?"

"The morale of the guards is now very poor. With Mussolini gone, no one knows what will happen next." He leant forward, wagging his finger. "It would need only a small party of determined men. A surprise attack in the dark, a gap blown in the wire fences —"

"You really think so?" Rick could not restrain the eagerness in his voice.

"I could do it myself. I have the men, I now have the explosive. I need only a few more things." Rossi counted them on outspread fingers: "Wire-cutters, grenades, automatic weapons..."

"Sounds a good idea. I'll pass it on."

They turned to talk of the general war news. Rossi was keen to hear what the BBC was saying. Rick told him. Still some bitter fighting in Sicily. Italian resistance half-hearted, but stiffened now by German reinforcements, a whole armoured division...

"No Allied crossing to the mainland?"

"No. But very soon now. Once we start, our troops will sweep up the peninsula like a fire."

"All the faster if bands like mine are operating ahead of them!"

Rossi took his leave. They had heard the slow bumbling of an aeroplane above the clouds. Soon the sun would break through and the guerrillas must get off the exposed uplands. The theft of the dynamite would have been discovered. The hunt would be starting. Rossi's followers took up the wooden boxes and filed after him towards the shelter of the forest.

"We're a bit exposed ourselves," Rick remarked to Charlie.

"So I was just thinking. What with these Carabinieri riding the range, so to speak, and a chance of being spotted from the air too. Now that our friend Rossi has stirred things up like this..."

"I'll explain to Andrea. We'll shift into the forest during the daylight hours, just come back to the hut to sleep and keep up your radio contact."

They followed that arrangement for some days. Then Lina came up with another plan.

"My mother says this is no place for the signori. You must come down to the farm. It will be quite safe."

Rick was tempted. But he hesitated, afraid that his personal inclinations might be influencing him too much. But Andrea chipped in. "Lina's mother is right. And my son-in-law is a sound fellow – be sure that he has considered the risks and can guarantee your safety. Their place is as isolated as this hut – but with much more cover all around it. You will be more comfortable. But I shall miss your company. And my good friend Carlo –" he chuckled and patted Charlie's shoulder – "who is so bad at Italian but so good with the sheep and the dog!"

So Charlie dismantled his aerial and they went. Lina had not exaggerated when she said that the farm was at the end of the world. It was a steep zigzag climb from the floor of the valley and one could believe that no stranger showed his face there from one year to the next.

The house and its outbuildings ran, pink-washed, with small shuttered windows and high barn doorways, along the base of a sheer rock face. Stepping inside was like plunging into a cool green twilight. One might have been beneath the sea.

Signora Scarlatti welcomed them in a kitchen that was itself like a cave. One wall had actually been hollowed out of the cliff, the others built up from rough blocks of undressed stone and irregular boulders. There was a red glow from the fireplace, where a pot hung from a chain, giving out a most appetizing smell.

The signora must once have been as pretty as her daughter. Now even the flicker of the fire was enough to show a face etched with deeper lines than mere weather should have brought at her age.

Lina had told Rick some of the family's history. Photographs reminded him. That would be her eldest brother, Paolo, grinning in his smart American clothes – he had emigrated to California, done well, married a cute American girl, and would never come back. And the boy in army uniform must be Emilio, the youngest, drafted to fight on the Russian front. He too would never come back.

The signora followed his glance. "By rights they should not be here in the kitchen. Their place is in the best room. But we are so seldom there. A mother spends her life in the kitchen. I like to have them with me."

"Of course," he said gently.

Lina was laying the long table, slicing a club-like crusty loaf, setting out glasses and a bottle of wine that winked redly at the fire. Her other brother, Matteo, came in from the stables, a stocky youth, as quiet as his sister was vivacious. Lastly her father arrived, a grave unsmiling man with a stoop, the stubble on his chin already flecked with silver. He took the head of the table, raised his eyes to the crucifix on the wall, and muttered a grace. Then, as they all sat down, he said simply, "It is good to see a full table once more. You are most welcome to this house, signori."

They had soup, a thick satisfying minestrone, full of shredded cabbage, beans and bits of pasta. Then came slices from a smoked ham dangling in the gloom above the fireplace. Almost all the food had come from the farm.

Afterwards the signora led them up a steep staircase into a shadowy low-ceilinged room with one tiny window, like an embrasure in the rock wall, giving a glimpse of the yard and the forested slopes across the valley. The narrow beds seemed high with their bulky feather mattresses and massive pillows. "This is the boys' room," she said, "but Matteo now prefers to sleep in another." Under the window there was an ancient oak chest. All the time that they spent at the Scarlatti farm they never opened that chest. They knew that it contained the boys' things – old possessions that would never be claimed but were private treasures, not to be pried into.

"You can understand," Charlie once said to Rick, "why these people aren't any fonder of Hitler than we are."

On that first afternoon it was Lina who showed them all round the farm buildings. They must learn the lie of the land so that, if the unexpected happened, they would know good hiding-places. She took them into the warm sweet-smelling haylofts, the white-washed cowsheds, the chilly wine cellar hewn out of the rock. She pointed out the thread-thin little paths, starting behind a pigsty or a stack of logs, that would lead them swiftly and unseen into the woods that crowded round, dense and mysterious, on every side.

It was obvious that she loved the farm, but it was the love, thought Rick, of any girl for a childhood home in which she had been happy. Matteo would one day take over their father's farm. Lina, without real regret, would take wing to wherever her fortune led her.

Charlie's immediate concern was to find a satisfactory place for his radio equipment. With her help he selected a camouflaged corner high in the roof of a barn, where experiment showed that he could send and receive messages without undue interference from the surrounding hills.

In the days that followed he was able to transmit several favourable reports from Rick, passing on news of Rossi's guerrilla efforts. The coastal railway track had been dynamited in two places, causing disruption to military traffic. A road bridge had similarly been destroyed. A petrol dump had been set on fire.

Rossi's group could do much more, he pleaded, if only they could be supplied with first-class arms and equipment. But the answers he received were vague. He wondered if Blair could have done better. Was it his junior rank, he wondered miserably, that caused his pleas to be disregarded?

One bit of good news did come through. "Take a look at this!" cried Charlie exultantly, running down from the barn. Rick peered at the scribbled sheet of decoded message that had just come through. *Tartan alive and well* STOP *still unavailable* STOP The message continued, mysteriously: *Official notification received usual channels Major McNish escaped April just recaptured sent Ponte San Cataldo camp* STOP

"Who's Major McNish?" Rick demanded. "This

must have been meant for someone else. Nothing to do with us. Except – oh, yes, Ponte San Cataldo is that camp Rossi's dying to raid. But what's Major McNish to do with us? If he escaped in April —"

"I'd lay a bet with you, Rick, boy-o – though we may never know if I've guessed right."

"What do you guess?"

"Our major saw that the only way of dodging the firing squad was to go along with their theory that he was an escaped prisoner. Suppose he confessed that he was? He'd need to prove it – but he only had to give number, rank and name. What if he'd fixed himself with those before he ever left the UK – sort of personal insurance? Suppose he knew of a real Major McNish who'd broken out in April and made it safely back? The War Office would know that. The Italians wouldn't – he'd still be on their list of escapees. So Blair says he's McNish and they look him up and say, fine, we've caught *him* at last. Everybody happy. Specially Major Blair." Charlie laughed. "He always struck me as a cunning devil."

"Well, if he isn't, you are. Anyhow, 'Tartan's' alive and well. That's the main thing."

"And only about fifty miles away."

"Might as well be a thousand, for all the help *that* is," Rick grumbled. "If only they'd give Rossi a chance!"

General news of the war they could get from the ordinary radio. Rick had the miniature receiver with headphones issued to SOE agents. The Scarlattis had their own wireless set, with heavy batteries recharged at the garage in the town and laboriously carried to and fro by Lina. They would all sit in the kitchen at night, comparing the various versions, Rick translating

126

the English language bulletins for the Scarlattis and the rather different Italian accounts to amuse Charlie.

September brought the kind of news they had waited for: the famous British Eighth Army, heroes of Montgomery's victories in North Africa, crossed the Straits of Messina and pushed northwards up the Italian peninsula.

"At last!" exclaimed Charlie. "This is it!"

Only five days later came the announcement of Italy's surrender to the Allies. Marshal Badoglio's new government had faced the facts. They could no longer continue the fight.

The next day Rossi appeared at the farm. He was tense and angry. "Now, lieutenant – *now* will your people give us the arms we ask for?"

"I am hoping for a definite answer. Any day." Sick at heart, Rick spoke as tactfully as he could. He had a nasty suspicion – and so had Charlie – that their SOE masters were finding difficulties. Some of the regular Army commanders were not so keen on guerrilla groups. They liked to be in complete control themselves, conducting the campaign according to the book. To them a resistance leader like Rossi was just an unshaven Bolshie, likely to muck things up at a critical point in their plans. The SOE had a lot of freedom, but to arrange an arms drop they needed the co-operation of Army and RAF alike.

Rossi seemed about to start one of his indignant protests. Luckily, Charlie came down from his radio hide-out in the barn, his face shining with good news.

"Just heard a bulletin, sir! General Mark Clark and the Yanks have made a big landing – at Salerno. And that's way up the coast, isn't it? Nearly at Naples. With the Italians laying down their arms everywhere we really should sweep up the country now."

"What's to stop us?" said Rick joyfully.

"The Nazis," said Rossi. There was deep foreboding in his voice.

FIFTEEN

For the second time Rick found himself forced, most reluctantly, to put a damper on Lina's bubbling optimism. Yes, he admitted, the Italian surrender was official. Their two countries were no longer at war. But he was not going to dance through the streets of Sant'Arpino waving a Union Jack.

"Look at the map, Lina!" he insisted. "See how far north we are from Naples." He ran his finger down. "The Allies haven't even reached Naples yet – there are no British troops, or Americans, within hundreds of miles of us. But there are no end of Nazis – and *they* haven't given in."

For the time being he was under orders to continue his mission as before. To lie low, stay where he was, send reports every night, await further instructions...

So it was that when a frenzied chorus from the farm dogs announced the approach of another unexpected visitor, Rick retired with Charlie to their hide-out beside the wireless transmitter.

There, after five minutes, a breathless Signora Scarlatti sought him holding out a letter.

"It is for you, Ricardo! From the Castle!" There was reverence in her tone. "A garden boy has brought it. He says he is to wait for an answer."

Rick took the crested envelope and tore it open, amazed. In a florid handwriting, all loops and curlicues like a wrought-iron gateway, the Contessa di Conza had sent him an invitation.

> *A day or two ago a little bird informed me that you were on a visit to this neighbourhood. It would be a great pleasure to meet you again and to have news of your distinguished and most learned father. I feel that the moment has come when it is no longer necessary for you to maintain your incognito. If, therefore, you would care to take dinner with me tomorrow evening...*

He considered quickly. To go – or not to go? He could surely trust the Contessa? Anyhow, she knew he was here. It would be more dangerous to refuse her invitation than to accept it. After all, as Lina kept reminding him, Italy had surrendered. He was no longer an enemy. The Contessa was quite reasonable in suggesting that he could drop his disguise. And – what ended his hesitation – he reflected that she might be very useful to him in his mission. With her influence and status, with her contacts in the neighbourhood, her goodwill could prove a valuable asset.

The garden boy from the Castle was waiting, sitting outside in the shade, gratefully consuming a slab of cake and a glass of wine. Rick wrote a careful note of acceptance. In Italian. Giving nothing away if, by mischance or design, it came into other hands. He did not show himself. The signora took it out to the boy, together with a tip as recompense for his long walk up the valley.

The Scarlattis were greatly impressed. It troubled the signora that Rick had no best clothes to put on. Lina would have liked to see him in uniform. All they could do was to press the cheap jacket and trousers that were his disguise, and see that his spare shirt was immaculate, his shoes polished.

To Lina the Contessa had been a legendary figure ever since she could remember. With her elegance, she personified the wider world for which Lina hungered. Since the war the Contessa had spent much more of her time at Castel Sant'Arpino. Lina had seen her at close quarters – in the piazza and the surrounding streets, once even in the Tre Corone itself which, like so much of the town, was part of her husband's vast estate. Lina had even spoken to her and the close encounter had not destroyed the magic.

"She is a fine lady – but also she is a human being."

"I know." Rick smiled. He needed no reassurance. He did not share Lina's reverence.

"She is a good woman," said the signora. "Nowadays she spends much time helping in the Convent hospital."

It was an evening when Lina was serving at the inn. They were able to walk down together in the cool of

131

the day. Lina, who as usual carried her high-heeled shoes in a bag, insisted on taking his shoes too. For the rough track down the valley Rick had to borrow a pair of her brother's rope-soled sandals. At the ruinous outer gateway of the Castle they paused to change into their smarter footwear.

"We're both early," he said. "Would you like to see where I used to work with my father?"

"Please!"

"I'd like to see what they've done to cover up the excavations – he's sure to ask me when I get home."

What had been a vast lower courtyard in medieval times had long ago been laid out as a pleasure garden with balustraded terraces and stairways, classical statues and ornate fountains. Sombre evergreens provided a foil to the pastel colours of the frothy pink and white azaleas, the clustered oleanders, the looping swags of pale blue wistaria. For shelter in the heat of the day there were slender-pillared loggias and cavernous grottoes yawning at the base of the cliff on which the Castle stood.

They walked over to the corner where banks of earth and corrugated iron sheets marked the site of the excavations. He pointed to a dark hole in the uncovered masonry of the foundations. "That leads into the hypocaust."

"Ah! We were told at school. The Romans had already a sort of central heating?"

"Yes." He explained how the floors had been warmed by hot air circulating from a stove. "The floors are held up by lots of little brick pillars. There's just room to crawl about underneath. Two or three feet head-room." He chuckled at a memory. "I gave my father an awful scare when I was a kid. I got lost

132

exploring down there. It *was* dangerous. I didn't realize – those pillars can collapse. I might have been buried alive."

She shuddered. "I am glad you were not! I think, Ricardo, you must have been a very naughty little boy."

"Father called me a venturesome little devil." He glanced at his watch. "I'll have to go now. Mustn't keep the Contessa waiting."

"And you had better not be seen with that Scarlatti girl!"

They parted. Lina flitted away along the now twilit terraces. He turned up the steep drive that wound through the trees to the Castle entrance, a weathered stone archway with carved griffins looking down superciliously from the swallow-tailed battlements. Beyond, a portly figure in black hovered on the broad flight of steps that led up to the residence itself.

He remembered Zanchi – who could forget Zanchi, the self-important Zanchi, who always insisted that he was not just a butler but must be referred to as the "major-domo"?

If Zanchi remembered the English boy, normally grubby but always well-scrubbed when visiting with his father, he did not show it by the slightest tremor of his bushy eyebrows.

"Good evening, signore. It is good to see you here again."

He spoke as though Rick had returned for yet another visit – as though nothing had happened in the four years since the last.

"And you, Zanchi!" It was an effort to inject the right degree of easiness into his own voice. He was a boy no longer, but a man, the Contessa's guest – a

133

British officer, if Zanchi knew. How much *did* Zanchi know? One was never quite sure. Zanchi must be addressed in precisely the correct fashion. He was a servant – he would not thank you, as a guest of his mistress, to treat him otherwise, but he would expect you to indicate, in the subtlest possible way, that you knew he was a terribly grand sort of servant, to be recognized and respected accordingly.

Coming from a very ordinary, free-and-easy English home, Rick had to make a considerable effort to live up to the grandeur of Zanchi.

So, remember for once not to shake hands! Zanchi's spotless white glove would probably have shrivelled at such a familiar contact.

The major-domo permitted himself only a deferential enquiry as he led the way to the Contessa's drawing room. "May I ask after the health of the *dottore* Weston?"

"He's very well, thank you. He was wounded early in the war..."

Zanchi hissed his regret and disapproval.

"He's fit now, but invalided out of the army. So he's back teaching his students."

"A great scholar, the *dottore* Weston! A savant."

The little Contessa was sailing forward with outstretched hand.

"Ricki! I may still call you 'Ricki'? Or have you been made a colonel or something?"

He grinned. "Not quite." He remembered to bow over her hand. She would have forgiven him if he had forgotten, but Zanchi would have been shocked.

"This is quite delightful!" She was as animated as ever, but she did not look as young as he remembered her. Strain had sharpened her features. She was still

134

dressed with that deceptively simple elegance which, his mother had long ago explained to him, cost the earth if it had been created in Paris.

They talked in English, the Contessa with her mastery of the words and a slightly comical inability to pronounce them. "I want the news — all the news!"

As they were alone, they dined in a candle-lit loggia thrust out like some seagull's nest from the castle wall, its columned windows framing the last of the sunset. A single footman served them. A simple meal, she said apologetically. In England, thought Rick, it would have been a banquet. Wartime shortages seemed not to have affected the kitchen at the Castle.

At first, until the footman left them, they kept to small talk. Rick's father, news of the Italian professors who had worked with him, the Contessa's hope that now the war was over it might be possible one day to resume the excavations... She spoke of her husband, the Conte, away on duty with some diplomatic mission to Portugal...

"Perhaps fortunately," she said with a meaning look, "in the present unsettled situation."

The footman served their coffee, then silently withdrew. "Now we can really talk," said the Contessa, and instinctively Rick braced himself.

How much could he divulge of his mission? How much could he safely ask her? He had already rehearsed in his mind the sort of questions that he was sure Blair would have put — the sort of information that would be of interest to headquarters, if only she was able to supply it. Before they could get started, however, the footman returned to murmur that she was wanted urgently on the telephone.

After some minutes she returned, apologizing for the

135

interruption. "I spoke of the unsettled situation. I might well! It is changing every hour."

Rick eyed her keenly. Something must have happened. But what? One did not fire questions at the Contessa. She was clearly going to tell him.

"That telephone call. It was from a very old friend – we were girls together. She is now a lady-in-waiting to the Queen."

"She was ringing from Rome?"

"Yes – but on the point of leaving the palace – and the city. She had to wrap up what she told me, but I took her meaning. As I say, we were girls together."

"I take it something has happened in Rome?"

"Decidedly." The Contessa's tone was no longer light. It had become grim. "The King has left. So has the Prime Minister – and all the government. The whole of the Royal Family is in flight."

"Flight?"

"She was about to tell me where. But the line was cut – suddenly."

"We can guess what this means, Contessa. The Germans —"

"Are taking over. It's what my husband always feared. Italy drops out of the war – but that man, Hitler, will not permit it! He daren't let the Allies occupy our country. So he will occupy it himself."

Rick remembered Rossi's forebodings. "Thank goodness your King seems to have got away in time! And Marshal Badoglio, you said? The whole government – and the Royal Family?"

"Yes. But where can they *go*?"

"I expect the Allies have a plan ready." Rick could only pray, silently, that he was right. Too often Hitler seemed to spring a surprise which caught the British and Americans on the wrong foot. "They will take your King and his ministers under their protection – if only they can get south and reach the Allied lines. They'll remain the legal government of Italy. Like the governments in exile that we have in London – the Norwegians and the Dutch and —"

He was interrupted by the entrance of the major-domo. Zanchi for once had forgotten his dignity. He was pallid, he came rushing in with a breathless apology. "Your pardon, my lady —"

"Zanchi! In Heaven's name —"

"These men. Armed men."

"*Armed?* Where?"

"Outside, my lady! I tried to ring the Carabinieri but these men have cut the wires. Their leader insists on seeing you."

"Insists? Who is their leader?"

"He says his name is Rossi."

Rick broke in. "You would be wise to receive him, Contessa. He is the leader of a resistance action group."

"I know." She laughed curtly. "I am not ignorant of what goes on in this region. One may live in a castle, but it need not be an ivory tower." She looked at the major-domo. "Tell this man he may come in."

Rossi, however, had not waited for the invitation. He walked in, a rifle slung over one shoulder, a bandoleer full of cartridges over the other. Wild faces filled the doorway behind him.

The Contessa sat in her chair. She surveyed them without blenching. "What do you want, my friends?"

"Arms," said Rossi.

"And how should I have arms to give you?" She laughed. "This place has not been besieged since 1559.

137

Oh, there are pikes and halberds and so on, decorating the walls —"

"Your husband is a keen sportsman," interrupted Rossi. "A shotgun is better than nothing."

"You expect me to give you the Conte's sporting guns?"

"If you do not, we shall take them. But I ask you, madam, not to compel us. We are entering a true national struggle." His voice was earnest. "It is all the people, rich and poor, workers and nobility, Communists and Catholics — against the Nazis." He wheeled round on Rick. "I tried to warn you of this. Even the King has had to flee or the Germans would have seized him. Tonight they are taking over everywhere. Milan is surrounded by German troops, an armoured column is heading for Florence. There are German parachutists occupying Rome itself."

"You seem remarkably well informed," said the Contessa.

"We have many secret sympathizers." Rossi smiled. "Not least among the telephone operators throughout the switchboards of Italy."

She turned to the major-domo. "Zanchi, bring me the key to the gun room."

He returned with it – laid, from force of habit, on a silver tray. She led the way downstairs by echoing flights of steps and passages. Rick followed at her elbow. Rossi's motley band trailed after them, some noisy and truculent, others awed by their surroundings.

The Contessa flung open a heavy door and pressed a switch. The light leapt upon the guns, oiled and polished, gleaming in their racks. Guns for shooting every type of game from wild duck to deer. Enough guns for a house-party of twenty, or more.

"And the ammunition?" asked Rossi.

She opened the cupboards. He ran his eye expertly along the cartridge boxes. Some he rejected contemptuously. "We are not going to pepper the Nazis with little pellets — they are not pheasants. We need something that will drop them in their tracks. Like wild boar." He pulled weapons from the racks, handing them out to his followers as they pressed round. Some equipped themselves with a heavy shotgun as well as a sporting rifle.

"Have you enough?" said the Contessa ironically.

Rossi did not smile. "No. Many more will join our group as the situation develops. But it may not be easy to pay you a second visit."

"I think my husband would not begrudge you his guns. If they are not used against the King."

"They will be used only against the Germans. And any Fascist traitors who side with them."

"Then I think we are on the same side, Signor Rossi."

He inclined his head. "I hope so, madam. Our class quarrel can wait until we have settled the other business. I am sorry that it seemed advisable to cut your telephone wires. There is no need to report the matter officially."

"No need?" For once the Contessa was nonplussed.

"You will find that the telephone engineers will be here first thing in the morning to connect you again. As I told you, we have many sympathizers — and not only in the exchanges but also in the maintenance departments! So you will find that the work is done without any request from you."

"You are very efficient," she said amusedly.

"In our work we are either efficient or dead." By

now they were back in the lofty entrance hall. Zanchi stood there like a man in a nightmare. Rossi went on, "I am sorry to have interrupted your little dinner party with the lieutenant." He too could be ironic when he chose.

Rick said, "I think, Contessa, that I should be taking my leave. Signor Rossi and I have things to discuss – urgently."

"I can believe that."

He thanked her for a most pleasant evening. The guerrillas had straggled out into the night, but Rossi hovered at the door. "I think we are going the same way, lieutenant. I hope that will be true now in another sense." Rick would have liked to linger, asking the Contessa some further questions, but, with this startling new development in the war situation, it was more vital to confer with Rossi.

They walked together the first mile of the wooded track. "You see now," said Rossi, "the Americans and British will not have an easy time of it. Hitler will pour his own troops into Italy. They will fight for every yard of ground. Everything we can do behind their lines – sabotage and disruption of every kind – will help the Allied advance. But I need more than sporting rifles."

"I will transmit another request tonight," Rick promised as they parted under the trees.

And, as he strode on alone up the path to the Scarlatti farm, he was framing the appeal in the most persuasive terms he could think of. Two or three hours later Charlie was tapping it out in cipher.

SIXTEEN

The Nazis never wasted time.

It was only two days later that another stranger appeared at the farm. This time the dogs gave no warning and Rick was caught in the kitchen, about to sit down to the midday meal. Scarlatti had met the man and brought him up to the house. The face was vaguely familiar. Rick remembered it from the crowd of guerrillas who had filed through the Conte's gun room. The rifle slung on his shoulder came from the Castle.

He brought a message from his leader. It was no longer safe for Rick and Charlie to remain at the farm. He was to conduct them at once to Rossi's headquarters.

"The Germans are in Sant'Arpino," he explained. "They arrived at first light. Their trucks are parked all over the town. And they have come to stay – the officers have taken over the Castle for their billets."

There was a shocked outcry from the Scarlattis. Lina exclaimed, "But the *Contessa*..."

The man laughed unpleasantly. "The Contessa will be all right. She will probably collaborate with the Nazis – the aristocracy usually do!" He turned to Rick. "There is no time to lose. You must get out of here."

"The Contessa would never give me away..."

"One of her servants might. In any case, the Germans are sending out patrols in every direction – purely as routine – checking on the district. Remember, lieutenant – if they are not looking for you, they may be looking for us."

There was no way to argue against that. "Come on, Charlie," said Rick, "you take down your box of tricks, I'll clear the bedroom."

"But your dinner?" cried the signora.

"I'm sorry," said Rick, "but I think we must go, as he says. We must remove every trace, *you* must forget that you have ever seen us – and you must all stick to the same story."

He raced upstairs. Lina followed, near to tears. She gathered up an armful of bed linen while Rick packed their few possessions and checked the room meticulously for any careless clue that might betray the recent occupation of the room. Charlie was no less quick in dismantling his radio equipment. They found him downstairs, suitcase in hand.

The Scarlattis broke into exclamatory farewells, but they were cut short by a new sound – the splutter of motorcycles in the valley below.

"Quickly!" urged the guerrilla.

"They can never ride up this track," said the farmer.

"You'd be surprised," said Rick grimly.

He gave Lina a last despairing look and followed the furiously beckoning guide. Charlie was already disappearing round the pigsties into the dense undergrowth behind. The motorcycles roared louder, the dogs gave tongue in furious reply. In such a din no one could have heard the fugitives crashing through the bushes.

Some way up the precipitous slope they paused, gasping for breath. Through gaps in the billowing treetops beneath them they caught glimpses of the brown track, the field-grey basin-helmeted riders crouched on their bucking, slithering machines. Then, as the engines stuttered into silence, Scarlatti's resonant voice could be heard, quelling the dogs. Brusque, guttural questions were shouted in German. The Scarlattis answered, loudly protesting that they could not understand.

"We can do nothing," said Rossi's messenger quietly. He led them upward. Rick sent up a silent prayer that no harm would come to the good people who had so befriended them. It seemed to meet with a quick answer, for almost immediately he heard the engines revving up again, the motorcyclists bumping down the valley once more. It must only have been a routine reconnaissance, to satisfy themselves that the track led only to one isolated dwelling.

The guerrilla seemed to guess the hesitation in Rick's mind as he stood peering down into the forest. "No, signore," he said firmly. "You must not go back. Who knows when the Germans will return? And Comrade Rossi expects you."

Rick did not argue. In one important sense this summons from the Resistance leader was a step forward.

They needed to be in closer touch. Rossi had been a mysterious figure, appearing and disappearing. If they were going to work together Rossi would have to trust him fully.

The forest thinned. They were clambering up a boulder-strewn gully which in the wet season must have been a series of spectacular waterfalls. Above them, sharp cut against blue sky and drifting cloud, a V-shaped nick showed where the torrent had bitten through the mountain crest. Soon, breathless and sweaty, they were standing on the sun-grilled upland.

Their guide did not allow them to stand silhouetted in such a conspicuous position. He beckoned them on, crouching himself and, as he led them forward, taking advantage of every hollow that would provide dead ground to screen them. For an hour they kept up a brisk pace, never pausing until they reached the head of another valley and were able to plunge thankfully into the shade of its woodland.

Another mile, following a dried-up stream, brought them to Rossi's camp. First the tang of wood smoke drifted up to them. Then the trees parted to disclose an open grassy hollow, almost encircled by sheer rock faces, pitted with clefts and caves.

"Very Robin Hood," commented Charlie. "Good choice, though. Hard to spot from the air. Anyhow, bomb-proof shelters all laid on."

It would be very defensible on the ground, too, thought Rick. An attacking force would have to fight their way up through steep woodlands like those below the Scarlatti farm and, as there, the defenders would have several lines of retreat to the heights above. Only the local peasants would even know that this place existed. Unless someone betrayed it to the Germans they were unlikely to find their way up here. And Rossi's men, he told himself grimly, had probably a short way with traitors and informers.

Rossi gave them a cordial welcome. Soon they were sitting in a roughly furnished cave, eating a belated dinner of mutton supplied by Andrea Alberti. It had been conscientiously paid for, said Rossi with a smile. "We steal only from the Fascists – and now, I hope, from the Nazis." He was relieved to hear that the Scarlattis had got rid of the German patrol so quickly. "Clearly they were not looking for *you*. If they had been, they would have taken the farm apart, stone by stone." But it would be better if, from now on, the two British agents joined him at his headquarters.

The meal finished, he showed them to a cave close to his own, and blankets and piles of hay were brought in for bedding. His keenest concern, however, was to help Charlie find a good site for his radio equipment, higher up the mountainside where there would be less interference with reception and transmission. He was clearly delighted to feel that he would now have a direct link with the British forces and would possess, in Charlie, a source of information monitored from many broadcasts.

In the next few days that news was mainly discouraging.

Hitler's generals held all Italy except the south. With their usual lightning tactics they had sent their columns racing down the motorways seizing strategic points and occupying principal towns. At Rome itself they had captured the airfields before the Allies could fly in troops to defend them. Outside the capital, Italian regular soldiers had joined with local partisan bands to bar the German entry, but they had been crushed ruth-lessly.

On the credit side the Italian fleet had slipped out of its harbours, run the gauntlet of the German dive-bombers across the Mediterranean and reached the protection of the British Navy at Malta.

King Victor Emmanuel had been able to set up his anti-Fascist government in Brindisi, now firmly in Allied hands. His government had now officially joined those Allies and – for what it was worth – were re-building an Italian army to fight against the Germans. Suddenly it had become every loyal Italian's duty to help the British and Americans.

Charlie had received new transmission instructions. The SOE had just established a forward headquarters in the heel of Italy, not far from Brindisi. In future his radio contact would be there.

"Sort of comforting," he remarked with a grin. "Feels a bit nearer." Not that mileage mattered in the ether. North Africa or southern Italy, it made little difference – the battle-lines were still drawn between them and their controllers.

Perhaps the worst news he picked up in those excit-ing days was the announcement of Mussolini's escape from captivity.

Charlie rushed into the cave to tell Rick. "They've got him out. You have to hand it to 'em, these Nazis."

"But how on earth . . ."

"The government thought they'd moved him to a safer place, high up in the mountains where the Nazis couldn't possibly rescue him. But the Nazis came down in gliders – and they had a light plane that could land and take off there. They whipped him away. Just like that."

"That's *all* we need," said Rick gloomily.

A day or two later their radio told them that Mussolini was safe in Munich with his partner Hitler. He had actually proclaimed an Italian Fascist republic to continue the war on the German side.

"He'll be a puppet," said Rick, "with Hitler pulling the strings."

Rossi said, "He should have been put up against a wall on the day he was arrested. Shot like the mad dog he is."

Rick could understand the cold savagery in his tone.

Rossi had grown up in the 1920s when the Fascists first seized power. Those who opposed them were treated brutally. "Gangs of Blackshirt thugs," Rossi recalled, "chasing us through the streets. Three times I was beaten up. Twice I had the castor oil treatment."

Rick knew what that meant. Massive doses of castor oil had been forced down the victim's throat. They weren't fatal, but the effects were bitterly humiliating.

Rossi had joined the illegal Communist Party. In the Spanish Civil War he had fought in the International Brigade against the Spanish Fascists who had risen against the republican government there. "A hopeless struggle we had," Rossi remembered, "but it seemed better to die on your feet than live on your knees." The horrors of that war had forged the man of steel he had become.

Rick found himself made welcome by the guerrilla leader for yet another reason.

Almost every day brought fresh recruits, finding their way somehow to the camp. Not all of them shared Rossi's dream of a Communist revolution. They might be liberals or social democrats, devout Catholics or fervent monarchists loyal to the King. Some had no political views, merely a hatred of the Nazis as foreign bullies. There were young men who had left home to escape being deported to Germany as forced labour. There were regular soldiers who had slipped away from their units when they were surrounded by German troops and ordered to lay down their arms.

They were united only by their desire to destroy the dictatorship, liberate their country from the control of the Nazis and get out of the war. Rossi found them sometimes an awkward team to manage. Rick's presence – no Communist, but a British officer – helped to strengthen his position.

Especially with Captain Bandini. Even in his tattered uniform, stained and crumpled after a hazardous escape from the Germans, young Bandini still somehow managed to suggest the debonair smartness of the crack Alpini regiment to which he belonged. Between him and Rossi, Rick immediately sensed a rivalry. Both had much fighting experience, both had qualities of leadership. But a chasm of loyalties divided them – Rossi's to Moscow and the Marxist creed, Bandini's to the King and to the Catholic Church.

Rick was a useful card in Rossi's hand. Rick too was a commissioned officer, with allegiance sworn – in his case – to King George VI. He was at the moment acting head – it sounded absurdly grand on Rossi's lips – "acting head of the British Military Mission" to this area. If Rick recognized this Communist as leader of the Resistance here, Captain Bandini must accept the situation. Which, gallantly and with good grace, the Alpini captain soon learned to do. A guerrilla group, to survive, had to be absolutely united. There was no room for petty jealousies.

148

Rick was able to include in his nightly report the news that the Sant'Arpino Action Group was not only growing fast in numbers but now contained several officers and men from the Italian regular army. This produced, at last, the response he had been praying for. One night Rick was able to rush into Rossi's cave with the glad tidings.

"We can have our arms drop next week! We've to choose a suitable site for it and send them the map reference."

"Thank God!" In such moments Rossi was apt to forget that he was an atheist. "Now we can do something effective – something on a big scale!"

SEVENTEEN

No problem about the dropping zone. Rossi had long
had a suitable place in mind: high up on the mountain
pastures, yet close enough to the tree-line to provide
cover for a swift get-away. No hazards for the pilot of
the plane, no clefts or precipices which could cause the
loss of the containers. Above all, an area that could be
marked out with farm lanterns or brushwood fires to
guide the pilot yet not be visible to anyone in the
countryside below.

Rick had only to identify the place on his map and
transmit the reference in his radio dispatch, with a
mention of other useful landmarks that could be spotted from the air.

The date, as usual, was dependent on the moon –

and the weather. But at this time of year the weather should cause no problems. Rossi grumbled at the delay of a few days, but Rick could do nothing about that.

"If we could have acted earlier," groaned the Communist.

In those first weeks after Mussolini's fall the prisoner of war camp at Ponte San Cataldo would have been a soft target. "A ripe peach!" Rossi declared. At that time the morale of the Italian guards had been at zero. With a little determined effort the defences would have burst like a peach skin and the inmates would have poured out with no serious attempt made to stop them. Now the task would be much tougher. German troops had everywhere replaced the easy-going Italians.

Rick could only sympathize with Rossi. It was, surprisingly, Captain Bandini who suggested a probable reason for the long delay in arranging for the arms supply.

"I was stationed very close to another POW camp at that time – I know how anxious the commandant was, for if the prisoners had tried to break out there was not much he could have done. He was very relieved when he found out that the British and American prisoners had received instructions, somehow, from their own generals – they were *not* to attempt a break-out; they were to stay where they were until the Allied armies arrived to set them free."

"Typical!" cried Rossi. "Typical of the military mind."

Bandini took no offence. For once he agreed with Rossi. "Alas, yes! The generals love planned disciplined operations – with themselves in control. They don't want hordes of escaped soldiers roving the countryside. They'd like to have them in one place, to be checked and listed, given medical treatment and rations and clean uniforms —"

"Administration! Paperwork! Unfortunately the Allied armies never arrived."

"And may not now, until the spring." Rick spoke unhappily, with a sense of shame that the British, along with the Americans, had disappointed his Italian friends. "They've hundreds of miles still to cover. And now that the Germans have taken such a grip of things —"

"And the winter will bog them down," said Bandini.

Rick could see now why his SOE controllers had shilly-shallied about sending arms to be used for a raid on a prisoner of war camp. They might have liked the idea themselves but it ran contrary to the policy of the high command. Rossi cut short the discussion. "Never mind. In a few days we shall have the arms we need. Then we can do this job alone."

His confidence was impressive. "I hope," Bandini murmured to Rick afterwards, "that he realizes what we are up against." He had seen a good deal of the German army in the last year or two. He knew their formidable equipment, their efficiency, their ruthless fighting spirit.

The date fixed for the arms delivery arrived. The moon, the weather were both right. Rick and Charlie set off with the reception committee – Rossi, Bandini and about twenty picked guerrillas – armed with the best of the weapons available. Besides their own pistols, the two British members had shotguns.

"I don't expect to run into any trouble," said Rossi, "but tonight's business is too vital to leave anything to chance."

It was a longish trek across the uplands. Their destination had been kept a close secret. Apart from Bandini, Rick, Charlie and two of Rossi's trusted lieutenants, no one knew where they were going or the reason for the dozen pack-mules and the miscellaneous collection of lanterns they were carrying.

Blair, thought Rick, would have approved. This secrecy was in line with SOE principles. Tell nobody anything more than he needs to know.

The group had gained so many fresh members since the collapse of the Fascist regime. Rossi could not vet them all for reliability. It needed only one traitor, running to the Germans, to ruin everything. So, more than ever, the veteran underground fighter was taking no chances.

They arrived in good time at the chosen spot, a clear, very gently sloping patch of mountain pasture, close to the head of another densely wooded valley. In quiet, decisive tones Rossi instructed his men.

"Bernardo, you will move down to the edge of the trees and keep the mules under cover. Send somebody down a little way into the valley, to give warning if he hears anyone coming up that way."

"Yes, comrade."

"Once the stuff is safely in our hands, get it loaded and away, *whatever* happens. The two Englishmen will supervise – they will know about anything that needs special care. It is absolutely essential that everything reaches the camp intact – including our two English comrades," Rossi added with a chuckle, "or we may not understand some of the gifts we have been sent." He turned to his other lieutenant. "Get the lanterns lit and placed in a big circle. About a hundred metres across. See that your men stand well back from them. When the plane has dropped all the containers, help

Bernardo's party to rush them down to the mules. Tell some of your men to put out all the lanterns and collect them. Gather up the parachutes. Remove every trace of the operation from the ground."

"Very good, comrade."

"You are the rear-guard. Only when the job is finished will you return to camp. If the unexpected happens – if anyone appears and interferes – you will take appropriate action. Make your escape – but slowly. Gain time so that the mules get clear away. Try to cover your own tracks, as well as theirs. On no account must we give away our base."

"I understand."

"If it comes to real fighting," said Rossi slowly, and with a hint of reluctance in his voice, "you must take your orders from Captain Bandini. But he will depend on your knowledge of the hills."

"And where will you be, comrade?"

"I shall be wherever I can be most useful."

The mules were led down to the fringe of the forest, the lanterns were set out in a ring of winking yellow eyes, a sentry was dispatched to the skyline to watch for any sign of hostile life on the rock-strewn pastures. Now there was nothing to do but wait patiently.

Rick peered at the luminous hands of his wrist-watch. Almost time. He hoped that the RAF would not let them down. The circle of lights should be easy enough to spot from above.

"Listen!" muttered Charlie beside him. The distant throb was unmistakable. "Punctual," he said approvingly. "A Whitley, I reckon."

The Italians, sprawling among the boulders, drawing on their cigarettes, had become silent, tense as Rick himself.

The bomber came over at a prudent height, a shadow brushing across the white disc of the moon. It passed, the sound of its engines muted by distance and there was a murmur of dismay from the guerrillas. Rick called softly to reassure them. "It will come back, my friends. They will have seen the lights – now they must lose height before they drop the parachutes."

As he forecast, the fading sound began to increase in volume again. The Whitley had turned. Now it was coming in, much lower, much louder than before.

For Rick these moments were almost unbearable. If this operation came off all right it would mark the first tangible success of his mission.

The bomber roared low over their heads. Dark blobs hurtled out, their fall slowing as the parachutes unfolded, drifting earthwards on pale wings that glimmered in the lantern-light.

"Wait!" he cried harshly as some of Bernardo's party started eagerly forward. "There may be another run!"

There was. The Whitley vanished, wheeled over the mountain tops, came in again, shedding more of its load. Charlie was flashing a signal with his torch. They could only hope the pilot had spotted the acknowledgement. A third time the plane traversed the marked-out area. The ground was strewn with crumpled parachutes, like dead moths. Then the bomber droned away southwards and the silence was broken only by excited voices and racing, stumbling feet, as Rossi's men rushed like schoolboys into the ring of lanterns.

"Like Christmas," said Charlie.

But the "stockings", they both knew, held nothing very festive. The containers were full of lethal weapons and explosives. And, as Charlie anxiously reminded Rick, there were delicate items like radio sets, snugly

155

packed in kapok. They must not be damaged in the enthusiasm of the moment. Rick shouted a warning in Italian. Crestfallen, the guerrillas began to handle everything with exaggerated care.

"But quickly!" Rossi insisted. He moved to and fro, seeing that the mules were loaded, hastening up the hill to check that every lantern had been extinguished and brought in, every giveaway clue tidied from the dropping-ground. Perfection was Rossi's watchword, perfection almost instantaneously achieved. "I want you all back at the camp before sunrise," he said.

And in fact they were, dog-weary but exultant. The mules had vanished, back to the undisclosed sources from which they had been borrowed for the night. Their recent burdens were carefully stacked, under guard, in a vacant cave. The morning air was strong with the smells of wood smoke and tobacco smoke and bitter coffee. Rick was suddenly conscious of his hunger and exhaustion, but who could relax, let alone sleep, until the supplies had been unpacked and examined?

As soon as he had swallowed his coffee and eaten a hunk of bread Rick got to work with Rossi and the others. Rapidly, but methodically, carefully listing every item, explaining when necessary...

Rossi and his lieutenants were delighted with the Sten-guns. Rick demonstrated how their three separate parts were quickly assembled and the magazine, loaded with twenty-eight rounds, clipped on at right-angles to the barrel. "You can fire single shots or short bursts. You have to make it short bursts – it fires at a rate of 550 rounds a minute!"

"There are only three magazines with each gun," Bandini warned the guerrillas.

"We'll hope for further consignments," said Rick. "Otherwise, the calibre's the same as the German Schmeisser M.P.38 – nine millimetres – so the ammunition is interchangeable. If we can get some of that off the Nazis..."

"We shall," promised Bernardo grimly.

"It's a grand little weapon. You can drop the Sten in water, you can get mud in it – it still works."

There were two bren-guns, accurate up to about half a mile. Their ammunition was similarly interchangeable with the cartridges of the standard Lee-Enfield rifle.

The other arms included pistols and powerful little hand-grenades. These could be thrown thirty yards and were as good as the bigger and clumsier German "potato-mashers" with their long wooden handles.

Weapons were only part of the delivery. After two years' experience in other enemy-occupied countries the SOE had learnt what was most needed. There were medical kits, emergency food rations, water-purifying tablets. There were stout boots in various sizes and warm clothing for the wintry conditions soon to come. There were tool-kits and wire-cutters. There were radio sets.

The Italians were particularly fascinated by the various devices for sabotage. Everyone knew such tricks as putting sand or sugar into petrol tanks to immobilize enemy vehicles. Much more subtle were the harmless-looking cans apparently containing heavy motor oil. "It's mixed with finely ground carborundum – that's really a polishing agent," Rick explained. "So it's abrasive. Any part lubricated with it will soon seize up."

They could all see the advantage of that. One of the

most useful things a resistance group could do was to hinder the movement of Nazi road traffic supplying the fighting line in the south.

There were high explosives disguised in ingenious forms that tickled Rossi's macabre sense of humour. Lumps of coal which, shovelled into a barrack room stove, would produce a far bigger fire than anyone intended. Plastic replicas of horse droppings which, scattered over a road, would destroy the first vehicle that ran over them.

Rossi saw an immediate use for these in the defence of their own camp. So far, they had had to rely upon the remoteness of the caves and the fact that this particular valley was covered with forest and contained no habitations. The track leading up through it was therefore known only to the forestry workers and was little used. A sentry was always posted, well down the valley, to give warning of danger. In future, if a German patrol were sighted, it would be a matter of moments only to lay down a protective barrier of these plastic explosives across the track.

"What thought has gone into all this!" said Rossi.

Rick smiled, pleased that at last the British had done something to win his admiration. He explained about the back-room boys of Baker Street, and how they could call upon the best brains in science and industry. "The SOE comes up with the problem," he said, "and these people work night and day to find the solution."

"They have worked well. With these devices..." Rossi did not go on. But the thoughtful gleam in his dark eyes suggested that his mind was racing ahead, considering how all this new equipment could be worked into his schemes.

Above all, his long-cherished plan to crack open the

prison camp at Ponte San Cataldo...

That dream, however, was doomed to be shattered before many hours had passed.

They were at supper in Rossi's cave when one of the guerrillas came in and handed the leader a crumpled note. Rossi unfolded it and held it in the lantern light. "*Damnation!*" he muttered with intense bitterness.

Rick looked at him anxiously. He had learnt not to fling questions at the Communist. Rossi would pass on information in his own good time. Or not at all. But on this occasion he made no attempt to withhold the bad news.

"So much for our San Cataldo operation," he said. He looked round the ring of faces. "As I feared, we have left it too late."

"Why?" demanded Bandini.

"Because, captain, the whole camp is being evacuated. All the prisoners are being sent off to safe custody – in Germany!"

EIGHTEEN

There was general consternation. Rick whispered the news to Charlie.

The sergeant let out an exclamation of dismay. "That means the major, then?"

"Presumably. If he's still there."

They had both clung to the hope that, if Rossi's daring project ever came off, Blair would be among those rescued. They had told themselves that it was a slender hope, but there had been at least a chance. Not now. If Blair had managed to keep up his pretence and had escaped exposure as a spy he would spend the rest of the war in Germany. Which could mean another year or two.

Bandini was questioning Rossi. Rick had to switch

his attention back to the general discussion in Italian.

"Have they begun moving the prisoners?"

Rossi consulted the paper he was holding. "The first train went through last night. At this moment they may be loading the second."

"And – you are quite sure your information can be relied on?"

"It comes from a Party member," said Rossi stiffly.

"And he is in a position to know?"

"He is a signalman. It is a little difficult," said Rossi with a touch of irony, "to move trains without the railwaymen hearing about it. Especially those who control the signals." Rossi paused. Rick could imagine how fast the brain was working inside that scarred and dented skull. "We have many Party members employed on the railway," he went on, "and many sympathizers. Railwaymen are a very close-knit body of workers. They have their own *esprit de corps*, captain, believe it or not – no less than the splendid soldiers of your own regiment!"

"I wish it were of equal military value!"

"Perhaps it may be."

"How?"

Again Rossi frowned at the smudged writing of the note. "My informant says that there will be only one train each night. As you know, captain, it is a single line most of the way, it is already heavily loaded and it cannot be easy to add extra trains to the regular schedule. He estimates that it will take four trains to clear the camp even with the prisoners packed close in cattle trucks. So there should still be a train in transit, perhaps the last, on the day after tomorrow."

"So?" Thoughtfully Bandini stroked his elegant moustache. "Do I begin to see daylight?"

161

Rossi's smile was more amiable than usual. "I think you do, captain. You are a soldier – and you are an intelligent man. But it will not be daylight so much as..." he chuckled, "moonlight."

"We could stop the train! Derail it or..."

"The exact details we must discuss – and very quickly. It is obviously impossible now to mount an attack on the camp itself..."

"Always a very risky operation..." Bandini could not hide the relief in his tone. Rick knew that the captain had always had his doubts about the scheme.

"But we have just time, if we act promptly, to arrange an ambush. If we could liberate a quarter of the prisoners..."

"It would be an admirable achievement," said Bandini, warming with enthusiasm.

Rossi turned to Rick. "If we might study that excellent map of yours, Ricardo? For the smaller details I can make a sketch. I think I know the ideal spot on the line where it would be practicable."

They put their heads together under the dangling lantern.

All the way down the Adriatic coast, from Rimini to Brindisi, the railway kept close to the sea and the main road mostly ran parallel on the inland side, just as Rick remembered it from that first night of their arrival. Any conspicuous happening on the line would be visible from that road – especially to lorry drivers in their high seats. And traffic was plentiful throughout the night because of the Allied air raids during the day.

"You had a place in mind?" he said.

"Yes." Rossi laid his finger on a point to the north of Sant'Arpino. From their own camp, Rick guessed, it would be about fifteen miles. "Here there is a little

162

ridge of high ground running down to the beach. It is nothing of consequence – except to our plan. The road runs over it – but the builders of the railway dug a cutting."

"So for that stretch the road and the railway are out of sight of each other?"

"For almost two kilometres. Also, the engineers chose this as one of the places where the line changes to double track, so that a train going one way can wait while another travelling in the opposite direction can pass." Rossi seized a pencil and began to sketch vigorously. "You see? There is no need for a derailment, which might cause death or injury to our own people in the train. If the train can simply be side-tracked and brought to a halt —"

"Which means control of points and signals," said Bandini.

"That need be no problem. There is a signal-box *here*..." Rossi drew a square at the bottom of his diagram. "Whether or not the signalman is sympathetic, he will be overpowered, bound and gagged. That is necessary for his own protection – when the Germans start their inquiry into the incident. We can operate the points and signals ourselves – we have several railway workers in our group. They will also cut the telephone wires. For the short time we need, this stretch of the line will be completely isolated."

"There will be an armed guard on the train."

"Yes, captain. But we shall have the advantage of surprise. The guards will be at the front and the rear – they will certainly not pen themselves in those trucks with the prisoners."

The trucks, he explained, being normally used for cattle, would not be locked, merely strongly barred on the outside. The bars could not be lifted by the captives inside, but would present no difficulty to their rescuers. While two detachments of guerrillas engaged the German guards at front and rear, others would open the trucks and the prisoners would jump down to freedom. The train could be emptied in a matter of minutes.

"And then?" insisted Bandini.

Rossi shrugged. "If we have dealt successfully with the guards we shall blow up the locomotive. But if the Nazis are still resisting we shall try to retire in good order – having given the prisoners time to get away."

"Yes," said Rick. "What about the prisoners?"

Charlie was tugging his sleeve. Charlie knew the gist of their discussion – Rick had interpreted to him in an undertone. Now Charlie was whispering urgently. "Our chaps can't just spill out into the darkness and melt away. It could turn into a shambles..."

"What about the prisoners?" Rossi echoed. "We shall have given them their liberty..."

"It's not enough," said Rick desperately.

"For most men it is a great deal!"

"I know! But you must realize..." It wasn't easy to stand up to a man like Rossi, but he had to force himself. "These men have been prisoners for months, some perhaps for two or three years. They may be in very poor condition. If they are just turned loose in unknown country, without food, without weapons, without more than a word or two of Italian..."

"They will be taken care of," said Rossi irritably. "One step at a time. I have first to make sure that we can deal with the Germans – we have only forty-eight hours to arrange this business..."

"Exactly." Bandini came back into the argument, supporting Rick. As a regular officer he had the same

164

instinctive concern for the men, the same sense of responsibility. Rossi had learnt his fighting in the rough-and-ready school of the Spanish Civil War, when heroic idealism had been mingled with hideous barbarity and the survival of an individual man had seemed nothing compared with the triumph of the cause.

For a minute or two they argued fiercely, talking at cross purposes. In the end Rossi convinced them that he would not forget the escapees. Men would be detailed to muster them and conduct them, in small parties, to the comparative safety of the hills. Those who were fit enough could, if they wished, join the Resistance group. But under present conditions, even Rossi had to admit, he had neither the weapons nor the food supplies to enrol a large number.

"They can choose, like anyone else who has escaped," he said. "They can try to make their way northwards to the Swiss frontier or southwards to meet the Allied armies – if they can slip through the fighting zone between. Or they can stay in this region – many of our people will give them shelter. We can take them to safe houses where nobody will denounce them to the Germans."

Rick had to content himself with these assurances. Certainly the attitude of the Italian people towards an Allied soldier would now be much friendlier than it would have been a few months before.

Rossi drew the conference to an end. "There will be many details to sort out. I have some urgent messages to send. Tomorrow we can talk further. Just now, however, we all need some sleep."

He ushered them out of his cave. Rossi, thought Rick as he got down under his blankets, needed sleep as much as any of them. Whether he would take any was another matter. You had to hand it to Rossi. He was a great organizer. And he never spared himself.

Next morning there was no sign of him. He had gone, said Bernardo, to "make certain arrangements". By evening he was back in the camp, his features drawn with weariness yet lit by an inner confidence.

"Things are going well," he assured them. "Better than I dared to expect. We shall even have a couple of trucks to help us make a quick get-away at the end."

Bandini looked slightly alarmed. "But surely it will be too dangerous to use the road?"

"Not the *main* road. There is a side-road branching off to Sant'Arpino – we shall meet no one on that in the middle of the night. Also I have spoken with my railwayman comrade. He confirms the times. A train went through last night, another is scheduled for tonight at the same time." Rossi's voice grew wistful. "We could have stopped *that* – our plan could have been brought forward with a little extra effort – but —"

"But?" said Rick.

"We can only play this trick once. If we stopped tonight's train we could not stop tomorrow's, which is to be the last. And the most important."

"In what way?"

"My railwayman comrade tells me that it will include two passenger coaches as well as the cattle trucks. That suggests that they have left all the officer prisoners until the end. Which means that, if we are lucky, we shall liberate all the officers who were held at San Cataldo." He smiled at Rick, "Perhaps even, after this long delay, I shall make the acquaintance of your famous Major Blair!"

NINETEEN

Charlie was almost mutinous when Rick said that he could not be one of the party for the railway ambush.

He took it as a slight upon the Air Force. "You think I'm just technical – nothing but a radio man? I'm a combatant. If there's a fight on, I can do my share. The Army always imagines that just because you're in the Air Force..."

Rick tried to pacify him. It was nothing to do with inter-service rivalry. "If you were in the Royal Corps of Signals I'd say exactly the same. You're too valuable to risk. If *you* get knocked out we've lost our wireless link – it means the end of our mission..."

"And suppose *you* get knocked out yourself?"

"At least you'll be able to report the fact – and if

167

they want the mission to continue they can replace me. I'm sorry, Charlie. *I* have to be there. For one thing, there's got to be someone who speaks English. It'll be confusing enough for all the blokes on the train, wondering what the hell is happening and what they should do."

"The major may be on that train. I ought to be there, lending a hand."

"Well, I'm afraid you can't be. It's my responsibility."

"Very well – sir," said Charlie sulkily.

Rick sighed. He hated pulling rank. He still felt that there was something faintly wrong about giving orders to Charlie, older and so much more experienced. And being Army himself made it no easier. But sometimes it had to be done.

Later, when the time came, when he was crouched in the sand with the guerrillas, waiting for the action to begin, he wished that Charlie, the good old dependable Charlie, a sort of substitute elder brother, could have been there beside him.

Other thoughts, confused and varied, whirled through his mind in that final tense hour when positions had been taken up, when the whispering had to stop, when – though conscious of invisible companions in the surrounding gloom – he was essentially alone under the remote, unsympathetic stars, with the monotonous lap and slap of the Adriatic wavelets just at his back.

He thought of his Sten-gun. He had fired one briefly during his recruit's training and a few rounds yesterday in the forest – ammunition was too precious for much practice. He still handled it gingerly, keeping it out of the powdery sand, praying that all they said of the Sten was true and that it was proof against most adverse conditions. A Sten *could* jam, though... Also – what was far worse – it *could* go off by accident. A shot too soon might give premature warning and wreck the whole operation...

This would be the first time he had ever been under fire, the first time he had shot at a living target. His mouth was dry. He mustn't let these Italians down. Or the prisoners they were trying to rescue. He wished he had Charlie's experience... "A piece of cake," Charlie would have called tonight's adventure.

It wasn't a piece of cake and Charlie would have known it, however cheerfully he'd spoken. Somebody was going to get hurt tonight, perhaps killed. Maybe quite a few people. And it was too much to hope that they'd all be the enemy. No one could be sure how things would turn out.

That was why Charlie mustn't be there. Rick himself might be one of those who would cop it... It occurred to him, more poignantly than ever before, that he might never see his father again... or his young sister Sally... or – and this was a new thought – Lina Scarlatti... That reflection was unexpectedly disturbing. He pushed it firmly away, resolved to face the immediate future with the optimism Charlie would have shown.

Everything was going to be all right. Rossi had it planned to the last detail. He himself knew exactly what he had to do. By sunrise, with any luck, he would be back at the camp, telling Charlie all about it over a cup of coffee. And Blair with them, God willing, swapping yarns about their experiences during the weeks they had been separated. If so, of course, Blair would be in command again from now on. In some ways it would be a relief to hand over. In others it would cost him a pang to go back to his old junior status. But Blair was the fairest of men. He would see that Rick had done his best to carry on, that he had achieved a good working relationship with this prickly Communist leader... Blair would no longer think of him as an untried beginner.

The minutes ticked away. If the train kept to schedule, as the others had done for the three previous nights, it would soon be here. To calm his mind he ran over the layout.

By now the signalman would have been taken care of, his box occupied by men who knew how to operate the signals and the points which would switch the train on to the other stretch of track. The driver would halt, assuming it was the normal routine for giving another train priority on the main line.

On the seaward side, where Rick was himself, Rossi had posted the men with railway experience – members of the guerrilla group and other volunteers still employed on the system but giving their services secretly for this night only. These, when the moment came, would take care of the train crew, uncouple the coaches where necessary and get the doors open to release the prisoners.

A few other men, on this side of the track, would be ready to deal with the German guards at front and rear of the train. But most of Rossi's force was deployed along the top of the cutting on the landward side. It was they who would launch the attack and try to engage the whole attention of the Germans, while the prisoners leapt out on the seaward side and were hustled along the ·beach to safety. There would be some useful cover from a belt of pine trees planted as a wind break to prevent sand drifting over the track in winter gales.

This was where he himself would function. His job was to get the fugitives going in the right direction. An evacuation exercise, every second vital. He would fire the Sten only if he had to. If the enemy did not realize what was happening on this side of the line, so much the better.

Was that the train? From southwards came the faint sound, soon becoming a distinct clicketty-click of well-oiled wheels. His grip tightened on the Sten. Yes, it was the train all right. Now, obedient to the warning signal, it was decreasing speed. He turned his head to the left, staring into the gloom. Here it was! A dark, gliding shape. It took the points, a giant snake moving sinuously over the curve that straightened then into the loop-line. It slid past him, came to a standstill, shuddered into silence.

The most ordinary, unalarming of events. After midnight, a train is side-tracked and halted, waiting for a more important down-train to have right of way. Nothing to cause a sleeping passenger to do more than jerk into momentary wakefulness, grunt, and drop off again. Nothing to arouse the suspicion of a German soldier. Even the driver, aware that he himself was operating an extra train, would accept the hold-up as entirely normal.

Suddenly a little outburst of Italian voices, loud in the dark silence. Rick's eyes swung to the right, towards the front of the train. He could see nothing. The voices were abruptly hushed. Nearer at hand, a figure started from the blackness under the pines and raced the few yards to the track. It was just where the two passenger coaches were followed by a long string of cattle trucks. Rick caught faint metallic clanks as the second coach was uncoupled from the first of the trucks. Still no reaction from anyone aboard the train. . .

Now the locomotive was pulling away again, very slowly, drawing the two coaches. The cattle trucks remained where they were. The locomotive gathered speed for only a few seconds, then glided to a halt again, leaving a gap of perhaps a hundred yards between the two parts of the train. Rossi had achieved the first of his objectives. The train was in two halves and halted. The German guards at front and rear were similarly divided. Even if the soldiers at the front were able to recapture the locomotive and get it to move they could do nothing about the main body of their prisoners packed into the trucks that were now uncoupled.

More shadows were flitting from the shelter of the trees, making for the train at well-spaced intervals. Unlike the first figure they did not dive under it, but pulled themselves up, groping for the door fastenings of the trucks. Muffled voices began to call from inside. The quiet of the night was now irrevocably shattered by the thump and clang of bars lifted from their sockets and falling. The heavy doors were opening, new shadows were spilling out of the trucks and dropping to the ground.

The firing started. Rossi's party was shooting from the crest of the cutting. From front and rear of the divided train the Germans were replying.

Rick's own moment had come. The men from the trucks were running towards him, some dazed and confused, hardly awake, stumbling. "This way!" he yelled. "Keep going! Through the trees – straight along the beach..."

There were guerrillas among them, pointing and guiding with a friendly hand, stammering their few words of English, keeping them moving in the right direction.

They'd be all right now, thought Rick with relief. They could not go wrong on the beach. There was a man posted to show them where to cross the railway track when the cutting ended. Someone else at the concrete archway that would take them, unseen, beneath the road into the open country beyond.

The guards at the rear of the train had just realized that, while they returned the fire from the guerrillas on the left side of the line, their captives were escaping on the right. Belatedly they were leaping out of the brake van at the back, loosing off their automatic weapons at the figures just vanishing into the belt of pines. Some of the guerrillas turned, crouched and fired back. This seemed to discourage the soldiers from quitting the shelter of the train.

There was nothing more Rick could do here. The other ranks were taken care of – which, he had been taught, was the first duty of an officer in this kind of situation. He ran forward to the front section of the train. It would be trickier at this end. The coach containing the officers might have German guards actually in the corridor. Certainly, according to Rossi's information, there would be a strong force of them in the other coach, next to the engine.

Crossing the open stretch between the two halves of the train he had a clear view, for the first time, of the battle raging on the other side of the line. Red darts of fire and stuttering flashes came from the automatic weapons. There was a brighter flash and a loud explosion when some stealthy guerrilla lobbed a hand-grenade into the midst of the enemy.

Rick reached the coach containing the officers. From the far end he could see a stream of dark figures cascading to the ground. The near door, however, was still locked or jammed and a head and shoulders protruded, swearing volubly in English.

"What the devil's going on?"

"The other door's open," Rick yelled.

"What? Are you *English*?" The irate voice was incredulous.

"Yes! Will you hurry, please? We're trying to get you all out of this."

Rick raced on. Vital to shepherd these men in the right direction. In his excitement and exaltation absurd phrases leapt to his lips. "All change! This way for the Piccadilly Line! Hurry along, please!" Yet they seemed to have the right effect. The bewildered captives were assured that there really *was* an Englishman out there in the darkness. The familiar phrases brought a prompt reaction of automatic obedience.

Now, however, there was a German voice shouting peremptory orders from the front of the train. It needed no knowledge of the language to get the message. In any case Rick heard an unmistakable English voice from the midst of the wavering escapers.

"It's no go, chaps! Best get back in the train. If he lets fly with that thing we've all had it!"

Grumbling, the officers began to clamber up into the coach. Others stood where they were. There was enough light for Rick to see that their hands were raised obediently above their heads. Beyond them he caught a glimpse of the German's helmet as the man covered them with his weapon. Rick's own Sten-gun

174

was useless in his hands. He could not fire without hitting the men he was trying to rescue.

There was pandemonium now. Staccato bursts of fire, single whining rifle bullets, the occasional explosion of a grenade... all this mainly on the other side of the track. Here it was chiefly flying footsteps, crunching the ballast of the rails, then muted as the fugitives from the cattle trucks plunged through the trees on to the silencing sand of the beach.

The guard was still shouting menaces. There was still a cluster of figures, hands raised aloft, waiting their turn to climb reluctantly back through the door of their carriage. Another door hung open, further forward, but no one moved in that direction, for the soldier barred the way.

In a few moments, thought Rick, the crowd would have thinned and it might be safe for him to take a hand. It would be a split-second decision. As soon as he had a clear line of fire... and before the German saw him standing there.

He was spared the decision. Suddenly, from the black oblong of that other open door further up the coach, a dim shape launched itself through the air. There was a cry from the German, quickly smothered. The officers started forward. Someone exclaimed, "Good show, McNish!" But to Rick's unspeakable delight the voice that answered was Blair's.

"OK! I've got his gun. Just keep going – I'll cover you!"

The other officers needed no further bidding. They were already melting away into the shadows. Those who had climbed back into the train were hurtling out again and racing after their companions.

Rick hurried forward to the major's side. The Ger-

man lay motionless, his helmet askew. Blair still strad-
dled his body, holding the sub-machine gun.

"This way, sir! It's all laid on —"

"Rick! Thought it was you!"

Blair did not turn his head. There was fresh movement at the front of the train. Several men dropped out
of the leading coach. More Jerries, thought Rick. Must
be. They shouted ferociously. "And you too!" Blair
grunted in reply and loosed off a burst of fire.

Rick followed suit. The Sten jerked and trembled
violently in his hands, spitting vicious death.

The guards went down, whether hit or taking cover
he could not tell. A few moments later he knew. A
sub-machine gun was stuttering in answer, the flashes
coming from ground level. But Blair was streaking for
the cover of the pines and Rick was only a yard behind.
He overtook Blair, sprawled in the drifted sand. He
thought that the major had merely floundered in its
softness, but he heard him grunt with pain and swear.

"It's my leg. They've nicked me. . ."

It was more than a nick. Blair tried to scramble up,
but collapsed again. Rick's hand encountered a hot
gush of blood. "Can you lean on me, sir?" If only,
somehow, he could get the major across the few hundred yards to the lorries waiting to pick up the rear-
guard when the show was over. . .

He had reconnoitred the escape route beforehand,
knowing that when the time came there wouldn't be a
moment to waste. Along the beach. . . across the railway track. . . through the archway under the road. . .
Could Blair somehow limp that distance?

But when the major made a second attempt to rise,
he sank back with a groan and as Rick bent over him
he seemed to have lapsed into unconsciousness.

He needed to be carried and Rick did not delude himself that he had the strength to do it. Blair was a tall man, heavy for all his lean appearance. There was no help in view, the beach seemed deserted. The stream of hurrying prisoners had ceased. The few Resistance fighters posted to guide them had now followed, thinking no doubt that there were no more to come.

In fact the show *was* over — for everybody else. The fugitives would by now have a good start in their escape through the dark countryside. As for Rossi and the party covering that retreat, how long would they wait before starting up the lorries?

Never had Rick been so near to utter despair. He could not leave Blair, yet he could not possibly carry him. And at any moment some of the German guards might come nosing along the beach.

Even now, as he knelt beside the major, he heard stealthy footsteps behind him in the sand. He looked round. Looming over him was one of the biggest men he had ever seen.

Everyone in Rossi's force had blacked his face as camouflage before the ambush, but even if this man's features had seemed familiar his sheer size proclaimed him as a stranger. His soft whisper, however, in an unmistakable American accent, was reassuring.

"Hey there, what seems to be the trouble?"

"He's badly wounded, I think — in the leg. If you could help me —"

"Sure! I guess this might be simpler." The giant stooped — and lifted up Blair in his arms — disdaining Rick's offer of assistance. A second figure materialized from the gloom, big but only normally big, limping awkwardly along the beach. His murmured enquiry identified him as Australian.

The first man was already following Rick. He turned to his companion, whispering huskily, "The kid reckons there may be a truck waiting. If *you* can make it?"

"You bet I can!"

"Joe doesn't walk so good either," the first man explained, "so we mostly stick together. Like now."

They came to the place where, Rick knew, they must cross the railway track. The two strangers turned at his low-voiced bidding, stepping over rails and sleepers with utmost care. The firing had died away, but there was still a good deal of noise from both sections of the divided train. Questions and instructions in irate German were flying to and fro. Torches were flashing along the slope above the cutting as the guards made a belated search of the ground for their attackers.

Now Rick could see, straight ahead, the hooded lights of traffic on the highway, skimming over the hill. He was following a narrow path used by railway workers. It led to the arched tunnel which provided a subway under the main road – and gave, at this moment, most welcome cover.

Half-way through its darkness they were challenged sharply. It was Bernardo. Rick answered and a powerful torch was flashed in their faces by way of check. Their shadows danced grotesquely on the concrete lining of the passage.

"Are there any more behind you?" the Italian demanded.

"I shouldn't think so. If there are, they'll have been picked up by the Germans by now."

"Then we can be off."

Bernardo turned his torch beam on the ground to aid the big American who was carrying Blair. At the end of the subway he switched off, but Rick could make out the vague bulk of the waiting lorry.

Bandini called softly, "Hurry, for God's sake!"

"We've a wounded man," said Rick.

There was a general stirring in the back of the vehicle. Friendly hands stretched out. Very gently Blair was lifted inside, set down and made as comfortable as possible. The engine started with alarming noise – though, as Rick quickly realized, it would hardly attract any special notice amid so many other traffic sounds. Vehicles seemed to be stopping and starting up again on the road above them. There was much shouting. The Germans appeared to be halting vehicles and trying to question drivers.

The lorry started down the rough lane that led inland. It showed no lights. Rick dared not call to the driver to go slowly for the sake of Blair. All their lives depended on a rapid escape from the scene. Only after a couple of miles did Bandini insist on a brief halt so that he could look at the wound and staunch the bleeding with a field dressing.

"It is not good," he said gravely. "I think this poor man must have proper medical attention – and without delay. It is not just a single bullet wound. He must have caught a burst of fire."

"But where can we take him?"

Bernardo, a local man, provided the answer. "To the Convent in Sant'Arpino! The good Sisters have a well-equipped infirmary —"

"But Sant'Arpino is crawling with Germans!"

"We must take that chance, Ricardo. The Sisters have no curiosity – no curiosity at all. They will not ask the patient's nationality. He is one of God's children, they will say. There is *something* to be said for religion," said Bernardo drily. He shared Rossi's hostility to the Church.

Rick had heard of other cases when Allied prisoners had been helped and sheltered. And here in Sant'Arpino the Contessa was a close friend of the Mother Superior and herself a voluntary helper in the hospital. There was a very good chance that Blair would not be betrayed to the Germans. Anyhow, both Bandini and Bernardo agreed that he would never survive the rough journey up to the caves.

They drove on. During the short journey Rick was able to question the two other escapees. The big man was Corporal George Wilson and, as Rick had quickly guessed from his speech, his black face was not camouflaged, but natural. The lame Australian was Joe Bateman from Sydney. He had the Cockney vowels that made him refer to his companion as "me mite", which in view of the black man's stature would at any other time have struck Rick as amusing. In the present grim situation, however, it was hard to see the funny side of anything.

"It will be best," said Bernardo, "if I take the officer to the Convent gate myself. I have my contacts, so there will be no difficulties. The rest of you can be dropped outside the town, as Comrade Rossi ordered. Have no fear for your friend, Ricardo. I shall follow you up to the camp when we have finished with the lorry and in the morning you shall know how things have gone."

TWENTY

No sleep for Rick that night. No time to rest, even after the final miles of foot slogging to get back to the caves. Every hour brought little parties of escapees, straggling in under the guidance of guerrillas. Charlie could help to welcome them, answer their questions and meet their needs. Only Rick himself could interpret between them and their Italian rescuers.

As a mere lieutenant he found it slightly daunting to deal with the senior British officer, a burly brigadier old enough to be his father. Even the stained and ragged uniform, with its unsightly coloured patches denoting a prisoner of war, could not hide the fact that here was a man of formidable distinction, probably with a string of medals to his name. But although the bushy iron-grey eyebrows shot up when Rick explained that he was acting head of an SOE mission to Sant'Arpino, the brigadier immediately put him at his ease.

"You're in charge, Weston. Just tell me what you want us to do. Only put me in the picture first – who's this chap who looks like a brigand chief?"

Hastily Rick explained Rossi's position and importance. "He's head of the local Resistance in these parts. You've got him to thank for last night..."

"And I shall! A damn good show."

"You'll appreciate, sir, *I* have to work with *him*. There's a limit to what I can do. In the end *he* makes the decisions."

"I get it," said the brigadier shrewdly. "Now – about our chaps. We organized ourselves pretty well in the prison camp. I was spokesman, dealt with the German commandant, all that sort of thing, and the rest took their line from me."

"It would be an immense help, sir, if we could carry on with that sort of arrangement. We'll have a talk with Rossi, shall we, and take it from there?"

"Fine. As I say, you're in charge. You know this fellow. I won't say a word to upset things."

By the afternoon they were able to make a guess at the success of the operation.

The brigadier knew that there had been fifty-three Allied officers on the train. No one had an exact figure for the other ranks, but it was somewhere between two and three hundred.

A hundred and thirty-four men, including twenty-five officers, had now made it safely to Rossi's headquarters. A few more might still trickle in. A large number, unspecified, had taken their own line of escape in the darkness and confusion and the guerrillas had been unable to shepherd them to safety. They would by now be scattered over the countryside.

"I expect some will be picked up by the Jerries," said the brigadier, "but there are a lot of very resourceful men among them."

"And they'll find most of the Italians friendly," Rick assured him. "Rossi is passing the word around. And in these parts his word counts for something."

A few of the men who had reached the caves bore slight wounds. It was likely that others had been killed in the shooting, or so badly disabled that they had been at once recaptured. The brigadier was delighted to have Rick's news that Blair was in a place of safety. He knew him only as "McNish" and Rick, preserving his practice of secrecy, did not tell him Blair's real identity or actual whereabouts. After all, the brigadier might himself be recaptured, so the less he knew about that the better.

Eyewitnesses testified that some prisoners had hesitated to jump out of the train. Some were physically unfit to manage the high drop or the strenuous effort that would be needed afterwards. Others, understandably, had been deterred when the German guards began spraying automatic fire along the line of trucks.

All things considered, though, Rossi had good reason to be satisfied with the night's work.

Now the next move had to be settled.

"Obviously we can't stay here," said the brigadier. "You can't feed us. You can't absorb us into your organization. And much as we'd like to lend a hand, we might be more hindrance than help, not knowing the country or the language."

Rick outlined Rossi's proposals. The escaped prisoners must rest for a day or two. They would be supplied as far as possible with clothes to replace their tell-tale uniforms. Then they could decide for themselves whether to trek southwards and try to slip through the fighting zone to meet the advancing Allied armies, or turn north in the hope of crossing the frontier into neutral Switzerland. They would be wise to team up in small groups for the hazardous journey. Guerrilla escorts would set them on their way and pass them on to trustworthy well-wishers among the population.

"I'll talk to my fellows," the brigadier promised. "We'll sort it out among ourselves."

A small number of the men were keen to join Rossi's group. They wanted only to get back into the fight against the Germans. A few of these volunteers were accepted. Especially welcome was an Army wireless operator, who would be invaluable as a relief for Charlie. Two others who stayed were the men who had helped to save the wounded major.

As the cheerful Australian, Joe, explained in his Cockney twang, "I reckon me mite here wouldn't get far disguised as an Italian peasant. He's sorta conspicuous." The black corporal had never let *him* down. Joe certainly wasn't going to leave George in the lurch now.

Rossi let them stay. He knew a good fighting man when he saw one. And both of them – but especially the black giant with his gentle manner and unfailing smile – were quickly accepted as comrades by the Resistance fighters. They were seen as living witnesses that this was an international struggle against the common Nazi enemy.

Within a week, most of the liberated prisoners had gone and the crowded camp shrunk to something more like its previous size. But Rossi's force was beginning to grow steadily. Besides the handful of new recruits from the Allied prisoners there was an increasing trickle of local men as the Germans tightened their grip on the region round Sant'Arpino. Their troops regarded the Italian people with a contemptuous hatred, as former allies who had let them down and changed sides. But they had scarcely any more respect for the Fascists who protested their loyalty to Mussolini, got out the black shirts and badges they had hidden when he fell from power and tried to curry favour with the Nazis who were now their real masters.

"Jackals! We shall remember their names afterwards," said Rossi darkly.

Sant'Arpino was full of Germans, billeted there or in transit to the southern fighting zone. A military headquarters occupied the town hall. Most of the Castle had been taken over as accommodation for their officers. The Contessa, it was said, had withdrawn to a private wing. She avoided her unwanted guests by spending more and more of her time helping in the Convent infirmary. There, using his own private means of communication, Bernardo was able to glean news of the British major: he was making a good if slow recovery, but would be disabled for a long time, perhaps permanently. He had a room to himself, very few people in the Convent even knew of his existence, let alone his nationality, and there was little risk of the Germans learning that he was there.

And even less chance, Rick realized, that Blair would be able to take charge of the Arpino Assignment again. Or of the SOE dropping in another senior officer to replace him.

Night after night he compiled and coded his report

for Charlie to transmit. Rossi was constantly sending out small parties to harass the occupying troops or sabotage their installations. The main railway line was now closely guarded and patrolled, but it was still possible to arrange a derailment or to damage rolling stock in the marshalling yards. Roads and bridges could be blown up, storehouses set on fire, petrol tanks filled with sand or sugar, parked vehicles stealthily lubricated with abrasive grease...

Joe Bateman, a garage-hand back in Australia, was especially useful on such raids and came back with triumphant and hilarious accounts of his exploits.

Rick chafed at Rossi's unwillingness to let him join in these adventures. "I know how you feel," said Captain Bandini sympathetically, "but our Red comrade is justified. You are too valuable to be risked on such operations. The attack on the train was different – a British officer was essential and we had no one else. But – remember your friend, the major! It could as easily have been you. And then...?" He shrugged. "No more arms sent to us, no proper contact with your people..."

The instructions that came back to Rick over the radio were equally emphatic. Carry on the good work. But do not expose yourself. No heroics. Headquarters, though not given to high-flown compliments in ciphered Morse, seemed very satisfied with what "Newboy" was doing. There were more parachute drops of weapons and supplies. But no one dropped with them. There was no suggestion that he was to be superseded by anyone of higher rank and longer experience.

Rick's impatience could not be controlled for ever. "I'm going down into Sant'Arpino," he told Charlie.

"I must have a look round for myself."

"But —"

Rick cut short the Welshman's objections. "I know, I know. But this isn't an operation. Just a casual recce. I shan't be noticed." He could see that Charlie wasn't convinced, but it wasn't his place to raise objections. "I know I'm not supposed to take risks," he said soothingly, "but it's also my duty to see things at first hand. I can't make a proper report if I sit in that cave just listening to what other people come back and tell me."

"Fair enough." Charlie's pursed lips crinkled suddenly into a sly smile. "You'll maybe run into Lina?"

"It's possible." Rick avoided the twinkling eyes. "I shall certainly have to look in on Lamberti. The major always said you couldn't beat an innkeeper as a source of information."

"And we should always remember what the major would have done!"

"Of course."

It was a Saturday when, as it happened, Lina usually went down to help at the Tre Corone...

He entered the town in the autumnal dusk. The curfew was not till ten o'clock, but he must be away well before then. The Germans were strict about it.

Sant'Arpino already looked different. There were German notices everywhere – direction signs, warnings, proclamations in Italian but signed by some Nazi general. There were tanks and armoured cars parked in the piazza, convoys of lorries halted for the night. Grey-uniformed soldiers thronged the narrow pavements, forcing the townspeople into the gutter.

Rick stepped aside for them, meek as anyone. He was not looking for trouble. There was no reason why he should attract notice in the Saturday evening crowd

187

– none of these Germans had ever seen him or would distinguish him, with his shabby clothes, black hair and bronzed skin, from the local Italians. Only once did he slacken pace and draw back behind a newspaper kiosk – when he recognized the distinctive swagger of Captain Collodi.

Yes, Collodi all right! Though he had changed his splendid Carabiniere uniform for the black shirt and riding breeches of the Fascist Militia. Rick smiled to himself. Trust Collodi to make the switch at the right time! The Germans had disarmed and down-graded the proud Carabinieri, no longer fully trusting them because of their allegiance to the King. With Mussolini at large again the Fascist Militia had been revived in the areas held by the Germans and Collodi, after a change of uniform, could safely strut again.

Luckily he was not bound for the Tre Corone. Rick walked on again. A placard at the door proclaimed that the inn was barred to the German rank-and-file. It was still open to civilians. He saw no German officers inside, but the hubbub and singing overhead told him that they had taken over the big private room on the first floor.

Lina saw him at once. He wondered if her heart, too, had missed a beat when their eyes met through the tobacco haze. She gave a tiny, almost imperceptible jerk of the head towards the doorway leading through to the kitchen and wine cellar behind. Then she went through carrying her empty tray and after a few moments he followed. She took his hand and drew him into the cold darkness where the wine bottles lay in their racks.

"Ricardo! This is most fortunate!"

"It's wonderful to see you..."

"And you too! But we have only a moment. The Contessa is wanting to talk with you."

"The Contessa?"

"She sent word to the farm. I went to see her at the Convent where she sometimes works – the Castle is full of German officers! I told her you were no longer with us, that I did not know exactly *where* you were, but that Signor Lamberti could perhaps get a message through to you. This morning she sent me this..." A paper rustled faintly as she pressed it into Rick's hand. "Go back into the bar where you can read it. If there is an answer, I can take it back to her tomorrow."

She was gone. He returned obediently to the bar and studied the crackling envelope and its contents. This time, though the quality of the paper was good, there was no crest and no address, but the flamboyant handwriting was unmistakable.

Dear Ricardo,
   You will be glad to know that your friend is improving slowly, but it would be unwise for him to receive visitors. But I am writing primarily on another matter. If this reaches you in time could you visit me on Tuesday evening? It must be Tuesday – no other day will serve. I have something I would like to show you. Please bring a camera if you have one suitable – it would save so much time. Young L. will show you the way to my present quarters.

This time there was no signature.

"Some wine, signore?" Lina was smiling down at him.

She took his order. "What time do you finish here?"

189

he murmured.

"At nine — because of the curfew."

"Then I will wait for you on the road."

"That would be... nice, Ricardo."

She brought the wine. He pondered the Contessa's note. He had a camera. Before leaving England he had been issued with a tiny Minox, manufactured in Lithuania, much favoured by the SOE because it used film only one-sixth the size of a postage stamp. One roll took fifty pictures and spare rolls were hidden inside his electric torch and even his shaving brush. "Suitable," said the Contessa. For what? Something to "save time". Could it be the photographing of documents that must not be taken away? Had the Contessa stumbled on something really useful?

Lamberti came over to shake his hand, murmur a greeting, and pass on the latest news. It was lucky that Rick had not been here two nights ago. There had been a raid by the German field police. They had scoured the town for men who could be rounded up and deported for labour — even as far away as the fortifications on the north French coast, the so-called Atlantic Wall. Anyone might be seized, from boys of twelve to men under seventy. Twenty had been taken from Sant'Arpino — the town was seething with resentment.

Rick memorized other scraps of information. Lamberti had noted various military units that had passed through Sant'Arpino, numbers of men and vehicles, destinations... Rossi could always use facts like that and in some cases they were worth including in his own radio reports.

Rick left without speaking to Lina again. But he was waiting for her under the shadow of the trees when she began her homeward walk.

"I know what the Contessa wants me to do," she said. "I will meet you in the Castle gardens on Tuesday night."

The German officers occupied the main portion of the building and there were of course sentries at the gate. But the gardens at the foot of the cliff were too extensive to patrol. The Contessa herself had withdrawn to the west wing, which had a private staircase winding down through the rock to a door that opened into the gardens below.

"It dates from the time of the wicked Conte long ago," Lina explained with a slight giggle. "He liked to come and go privately."

"I bet!"

"It is convenient now for the Contessa. She can go in and out of her own home without having to pass a German sentry. And so can you – on Tuesday!"

She begged him to go up to the farm with her and spend the night in his old room – her parents would be delighted to see him again. But he thought of Charlie, waiting to transmit his usual report in the small hours and of other emergencies that might have arisen at the camp. So, regretfully, they parted and he set off on the much longer walk to the valley of the caves. Tuesday was something to look forward to.

It was strange how, despite danger and duty and all the pressures of waging this underground war, there was still time to think about such things.

TWENTY-ONE

Lina met him in the shadow of the crumbling outer ramparts that enclosed the pleasure gardens. The Castle loomed black against a lemon-yellow western sky as the last of the sunset drained away behind the mountains.

The gardens stretched, deserted, to the foot of the cliff. One old man, with his dog on a lead, was hobbling painfully homewards. "Let us walk closer together," Lina whispered. "It will look more natural. Perhaps you should take my arm?"

But he took her hand.

A dense clump of evergreens masked a winding path and some steps, at the base of the rock. At the top, deep in a recess, was a nail-studded door. Lina slipped her hand out of his, fishing for a key. The door swung back silently. She pushed him gently in front of her, closed the door and pressed a switch. A light came on at the first turn of the staircase spiralling above their heads.

They were both a little breathless when they finally got to the top and found themselves in the hall of what looked like a modern flat. The Contessa greeted Rick warmly, apologizing for her workaday dress. "I have been helping at the Convent — working like a dog! Your major is very irritable, so you may guess that he is getting better. He sends you his best wishes. It was his suggestion that I should try to make contact with you." She led them into a drawing room, waving them to seats on a sofa and pouring them little glasses of vermouth. Lina accepted these courtesies rather shyly. For a peasant's daughter it was a new experience to sit down, let alone drink, with a contessa. How the war had changed everything!

"Now, to business," said the Contessa briskly. "There is a terrible fellow among these detestable Nazis — he has taken over my husband's study for his office. He demanded the key — the key of my husband's study, Ricki! I ask you — the *insolence*. I had to give it him. These Hitlerites have their jackboots on our necks. We are helpless. Naturally —" she smiled maliciously — "I did not tell the fool that I had another key."

"Naturally, Contessa." Rick waited eagerly, hoping that his guess about documents would prove correct.

"Tonight this creature is away, attending some conference. He would go mad if he came back and found anything missing from his files. But he will not. All will be back in place. You have brought a camera?"

She rose, drew on a pair of gloves and unlocked a

cabinet. She spread out a number of military files. "Wait!" She disappeared and came back with a pair of rubber gloves. "They will be a tight fit for you! But better than leaving finger prints."

"But you said that the officer would not know..." Lina burst out, then checked herself respectfully.

"True, my dear — but he may come to wonder in days to come, if Signor Weston can make use of all this information. As his major thinks he may!"

Leafing through the typewritten documents Rick saw at once that he might. He knew little German, but enough to grasp the possibilities. One item was a complete list of army units stationed in the region, identifying each, with precise numbers and location. An accompanying document showed on which days of the week the rations were delivered to them and at what times, with the itinerary to be followed by the supply trucks.

Here alone Rossi would find endless scope for ambushes, mined roads and other acts of sabotage. There were several members of the Resistance group who had fluent German and could translate the other, more difficult papers.

The photography took a long time. He had not enough film for everything. He had to decide swiftly on what looked most useful, ignore many sheets that did not. In the distance he could hear, through the thick castle walls, lusty singing from the officers' mess.

The Contessa winced. "Those ghastly Nazi songs! Every night the same. When they have had dinner and the drink is flowing. At least they are occupied. I shall not meet any of them when I take all this stuff back to my husband's study."

At last the camera ceased to click. The ornate little

clock chimed. "Heavens! It is ten!" cried Lina in dismay. "The curfew!"

"You must go at once," said the Contessa. "Go quietly – keep well clear of the drive and the gates where the sentry stands. You will meet no one in the gardens."

She hurried them down the spiral stairs. As they let themselves through the door at the bottom Lina whispered, "It has been useful, yes? It has been worthwhile?"

"I'll say so! It'll give Rossi a clear picture. He'll be able to spread disruption all over the district."

They crept out into the coolness of the night. They risked no more whispering. But as they descended from one terrace to another a broken step made Lina stumble and utter a little cry. She was unhurt, however, and they went on again, groping their way even more cautiously. They reached the centre of the gardens where the great baroque Fountain of Neptune rose massively against the stars. It was then that a blinding white light flashed in their faces and a harshly rasped command brought them to a halt.

You did not need to know much German to get the message. They were breaking the curfew. They were to stand still – or else. Rick caught the words "guard house" and "under arrest".

Suppose they were searched, the miniature camera discovered? No, decidedly, a visit to the guard house was not on.

"I will show you my papers," he offered politely in Italian. It seemed a natural enough gesture to reach for his inside pocket. But the sentry repeated, impatiently, "The guard house!" Rick pulled out not his identity card but a fountain pen and held it up in the torch beam. The soldier snorted, clearly thinking he was being offered a bribe. And Rick spurted the tear gas into his face, ducking the wild shot that passed over his head as the man cried out chokingly and staggered back, dropping the torch.

"*Run!*" gasped Rick. Lina ran. He hurled himself upon the reeling figure in front. His training in unarmed combat had been sketchy. In theory he had learnt several gruesome methods of noiseless homicide, but he did not try them. The German was down, temporarily blinded, gasping for breath. His helmet had rolled away. Rick seized his cropped head and bumped it energetically several times on the paving. This had a quietening effect upon the soldier.

Rick wasted no more time on him. He straightened up. He was not sure which way Lina had gone. But she had a good start and had known this maze of paths since childhood. The medieval wall had a dozen ruinous gaps. He could only pray that she was clear by now, for an almighty hullabaloo was starting in the distance. That shot had been heard. Heavy boots crunched on the gravel, lights bobbed along the terraces.

For the moment he was himself confused. The whiff of tear gas had left enough lingering fumes to make his own eyes smart. Some had invaded his lungs just when he needed all his breath.

He was tempted to crouch behind a balustrade while he recovered. But dare he lose time? The Castle guard might be small, but a telephone could bring instant reinforcements from the town. A sentry attacked – by a mysterious assailant equipped with tear gas, not a usual thing to take with you to meet your girlfriend. The Germans would go through the gardens with a toothcomb.

It sounded as though they were already extending a cordon along the outer wall. He had to think fast. No good retreating to the Contessa's private door. It was locked and if he banged on it the Germans would hear him long before the Contessa did. And it was unthinkable to involve her. If they learnt what she had done they would shoot her as cheerfully as they would shoot him.

Impossible to turn back, suicide to run towards those flashing torches, no safer to stay where he was. A military truck was roaring up the long avenue. Fresh troops would tumble out, automatic rifles at the ready.

Suddenly he thought of the excavations over to his left. In themselves they offered no better cover than the gardens. They were just shallow pits, grass-grown heaps of earth, footings of ancient masonry that rose only inches above ground level.

But – the hypocaust! The dark dank world beneath the tiled floors of the villa, once warmed from a furnace stoked by patient slaves... He had hidden there before, been scolded because of the risk of being buried alive by an earth fall. But what was *that* risk now, compared with capture?

It was rough going in the gloom. But he could recall the layout of the site as the Italian professors and his father had patiently uncovered it, drawing their plans and knocking in their pegs. He found the low entrance, knelt and wormed his way inside. Now he dared use his own torch, see how much head room there was, avoid bumping into the stumpy little columns that supported the floors above.

A new sound. It reached him faintly here in the bowels of the earth, muted by the mass of soil and masonry that covered him. Hell! They must have brought tracker dogs from the town.

Suddenly his refuge had become a trap. The dogs, uninterested in Romans and ruins, would follow their noses to the living modern man. They'd be taken to the scene of his struggle with the German soldier, they'd be laid on his scent and it would lead them infallibly here. He could imagine them, snouts thrust into the yawning entrance, straining on the leash, growling, hackles raised.

Their handlers would understand. They could dig him out for questioning – or they could send in their beastly dogs – or they could simply lob a grenade into the hole. One way or another, he was done for.

Blair had once said, half jokingly, "If you ever have dogs on your trail I believe there's a good way to bamboozle them. Pee! It's supposed to confuse them utterly. Never had the chance to test the theory myself."

Try anything once, thought Rick grimly.

He backed out of the hole and stumbled away to the point where he had entered the excavation area. Torches were already winking round the Fountain of Neptune. He could hear the hysterical rumpus of the dogs.

He did as Blair had suggested. Then he fled back and crawled as far inside the hypocaust as he could get. He lay in the musty blackness, heart wildly pumping. Even there the cry of the questing dogs reached him, now quite near. He could hear men shouting, at first encouraging the animals, then irritably rebuking them.

He could imagine the confusion at the spot where he had stood a few minutes earlier. The dogs circling and sniffing, then stimulated by some reflex to lift a leg themselves... after which, according to Blair, they'd be too muddled to distinguish the scent of their quarry again.

Certainly the hubbub was fading as their disgusted handlers led them away. Some men remained for a little while longer. Boots thudded on the antique paving, voices rang out in question and answer, but soon these also ceased. Silence fell. The silence, thought Rick as he lay there, of the grave.

TWENTY-TWO

At least, Rick consoled himself, Lina had got clear.

In this, however, he was mistaken. She had flung herself flat when the first army truck came roaring up the poplar avenue, but the second driver had jammed on his brakes, soldiers had jumped out and she had been roughly dragged aboard.

Much later Rick was to learn the story of what followed.

In the guard house, questioned in halting Italian, she stuck to her innocent-sounding excuse. "I had been with a boy, we lost count of the time – you know how it is, captain!"

She had to produce her identity card. "And your sweetheart's name?" demanded the duty officer.

That was awkward, she pleaded. "My parents disapprove of him. I am forbidden to see him. It will make trouble if —"

"The young man is already in trouble," the German reminded her bluntly. "We also disapprove of him! And of anyone who assaults one of our soldiers."

"He meant no harm! He panicked!"

"He sprayed a noxious substance in the soldier's face. Will you tell us it was a perfume — intended for you? If you withhold his name we can only think the worst."

In despair she chose the commonest name she could think of, impossible to check quickly. She must play for time. "He is such a *gentle* boy. I have never known him behave like that."

"I should hope not, signorina."

A man marched in, stamped and saluted. She heard the ominous word, "Gestapo". Her heart sank.

Were *they* being brought into it? She knew that, as the Nazis poured more army divisions into Italy, the secret police had come in with them. They were even here in Sant'Arpino.

"You are to be interrogated further in the Castle," said the officer.

The town clock struck midnight as they marched her up through the inner courtyard. It had been two hours! But, she thought thankfully, they had not caught Ricardo. Somehow he had eluded them.

She was taken upstairs into a drab room stripped of its one-time elegance, uglified into an office with naked light bulbs and typewriters. There was a man behind the desk, young, muscular, good-looking. Pink-faced, fair-haired, he would have passed for an Englishman. At any other time she could have found him attractive.

201

It was the sight of a second man that dismayed her: Collodi.

The Gestapo officer noted the look of recognition that flashed between them. In hesitant Italian he asked, "You know this girl?"

"I do."

"That will simplify matters. What do you know of her?"

"A peasant's daughter. Nothing against her – until a few months ago."

"And then?"

"There was a public disturbance. A mob broke into my headquarters. This girl was one of the ringleaders."

The Gestapo man looked at Lina with interest. But the blue eyes were ice cold and the interest was not of the kind that she welcomed. Something warned her that he would not respond to feminine charm. He turned back to Collodi. "And what happened?"

"The younger stranger was let out."

"Ah! One of the men you now think were British spies?"

"I am sure of it. It was common talk in the town afterwards. But I had no idea where he had gone – and in the utter confusion of those weeks – " Collodi was trying to justify himself – "when your people took over, their first act was to disarm the Carabinieri. I was left with no position, no influence —"

"A misfortune you quickly remedied – " the German did not hide his sneer – "by putting on a black shirt."

"I joined the Fascist Militia, yes – to serve our common cause." A fine pair, these two, thought Lina. "Perhaps I can assist you now," Collodi went on. "The young man who attacked the sentry tonight. The description fits one of the two I interrogated in July."

202

"Indeed?" The German adopted a friendlier tone. "Then, as you know something already of this affair, I will ask you to conduct the interrogation. I find these regional dialects somewhat difficult to understand."

Collodi's self-esteem was restored. He cleared his throat and addressed Lina with a pompous air. "You must understand, signorina, you are in a very serious position. Suppose that sentry had been killed. An order has been issued – for every German soldier killed in this way, ten members of the local population will be chosen by lot and executed."

"I have heard." She tossed her head. "It is barbarism."

He ignored her defiance. "Fortunately, no one was killed. But – what is more important – this young man is a British spy. It is your duty as an Italian to denounce him. An enemy of your country."

The real enemy of her country, she thought fiercely, was the blond brute watching her coldly across the desk. And Collodi himself, the jackal, doing his dirty work for him.

"If you help us now," said Collodi suavely, "much can be forgiven. It is easy for a girl's head to be turned by a good-looking young man. She can be led into folly."

She glowered silently. What did he take her for?

Systematically he began his questioning. He took her back to the night of the man's rescue from the cell. She had seen him again – obviously. Where had he been hiding?

She shook her head to every question. He changed his tack. Did she know anyone in the so-called Resistance? "A gang of Communists and other riff-raff, helping the Americans and the British! Traitors!"

"I have no friends who are traitors."

The Gestapo man broke silence at last. "It is late. We shall continue this in the morning. It may help her memory if she has a few hours to reflect."

She was taken down the corridor to another room, handed an army blanket and locked in. Remembering Rick's attempted escape from the Carabinieri, she went to the window. It was high above the courtyard. No chance whatever.

What an inncoent I am, she thought miserably, what a poor liar! In her happy childhood she had had little practice. Too late now. In those first weeks after Mussolini's downfall it had been common talk in Sant' Arpino that there was a British officer in the hills. Collodi knew. And the Gestapo man could see that she was involved. She could not talk herself out of it. Only stay stubbornly silent.

Alone in the darkness she prayed fervently. For herself – and for Ricardo. Would he guess what had happened? She hoped he would never reproach himself. He had risked his life to give her a better chance of getting away.

Her thoughts turned to the Contessa, asleep no doubt in her own wing of the Castle. Only in the morning would she hear that a local girl had been arrested for breaking curfew. She would be unable to do anything. Once a person was turned over to the Gestapo, nobody could. Hitler had given the secret police a free hand. Even a German general had to bow to them.

She thought of Collodi, a somewhat bedraggled and deflated peacock now, and of the inhuman blond German with his cold gaze. "Mother of God," she whispered, "grant me courage not to betray my friends."

She drifted at last into a troubled sleep, waking to the clumping entrance of the guard with coffee and bread. He escorted her to a bathroom and waited outside, his foot planted to prevent her bolting the door. There seemed to be no women in this part of the building.

Soon she was standing in front of the desk again. The German took over the interrogation, Collodi breaking in only to help with the interpreting. The same questions and answers were repeated wearisomely, either to trap her into a slip or to exhaust her.

Once she said, "In Italy a woman is not kept standing like this. She is at least offered a chair." She might as well have appealed to a brick wall. That she was a woman – a pretty girl even – meant nothing to the Gestapo man. It was Collodi who flushed.

Coffee arrived. Only two cups, naturally. After the swill she had been given for breakfast the fragrance was tantalizing.

Collodi lit a cigar. "The Führer neither smokes nor drinks," said the German pointedly. Collodi rolled his eyes heavenwards and stubbed out his cigar. "Do you indulge in *no* normal pleasures?" he ventured to enquire.

The ice-blue eyes were unblinking. "My duty is my pleasure." The interrogation started again. Lina answered only, "I do not know," or "I do not remember." At length the Gestapo man said, "I think the time has come to assist your memory."

Her chin tilted in defiance. "Whatever you do to me . . ."

"You think I would lay hands on you?" His expression changed to one of unspeakable disgust. "I assure you, you will suffer no violence. It is not my way."

She wilted under those eyes. It was as though she repelled him almost as much as he repelled her.

"In the end you will be glad to talk freely. It is just a matter of time." His laugh was a disturbing sound. "You wished to sit down?"

"Please. I am very tired."

"Give her that chair, captain." He opened a drawer, produced a length of cord. "Tie her to it." Collodi began to excuse himself, but he was cut short. "Kindly do as I say. As I told her, I have no wish to lay a finger on her." Reluctantly the Italian obeyed. "The hands behind the back of the chair, the ankles secured to the legs. You are comfortable, signorina?"

"Yes," she said faintly.

"I am afraid you will have to remain like this until your memory improves."

Remorselessly he resumed his questions. After an hour or two she was forced to whisper an embarrassed request. Collodi sprang up but the German waved him down again. "Not now, captain."

"But – I think you do not understand —"

"I understand perfectly. But I warned her. She will remain tied to that chair until she decides to talk."

Lina bit her lip hard. This interrogation could not go on much longer. Even this monster would want his midday meal.

And soon, to her intense relief, he rose. "Until three o'clock then," he told Collodi.

The Italian wavered in the doorway. She cried out in desperation. "Beat me if you wish! But in Heaven's name —"

"Until three o'clock," the German repeated. It was hard to say whether Collodi's embarrassment was any less than Lina's. He walked out without a backward glance. The key clicked behind them. She wrestled madly with the cord that held her. Tears came. She shook uncontrollably. Then she huddled moaning in the chair, overwhelmed by her misery.

The dreadful day wore on. Afternoon changed to evening. Collodi sat ashen-faced, horrified but powerless to protest. She could almost have pitied him, but she could pity only herself. She had braced herself to face torture, but she could never have imagined this humiliation. It turned her into a helpless baby, it reduced her to the level of a caged animal. Inwardly her soul cried out, "But I am *not* a baby! I am *not* an animal!" But no audible cry must slip out to tell the Gestapo man how near he was to winning. "Mother of God," she prayed, "give me endurance!"

Drink was held up to her, and food, but she shook her head. Not if they would not untie her, let her move from the chair.

The German remarked, "I have known men stand this even longer. But I should have thought that a young woman..."

Collodi choked incoherently. Then he leant forward earnestly, forcing himself to meet Lina's anguished eyes. "Signorina, I beg of you – give up this obstinacy."

"I can tell him nothing."

The German said, "We can go on all night. I have often done so."

Outside, the sky darkened. A blank-faced orderly came in and arranged the black-out. With the window covered the room became even more stuffy, the shameful smell more noticeable.

"Your family will be wondering what has happened to you," said her tormentor. "They know nothing – yet. But if you will not co-operate they too will be brought in for questioning."

She had dreaded this. How much longer could she hold out against this man? How could one pray not to betray one's friends when the alternative was to destroy one's family? She pictured her mother at this fiend's mercy...

He seemed content to leave the fear festering in her mind. "I can wait – a little longer," he assured her.

Did this creature never sleep himself? Would he leave her like this until another day?

There was a faint noise outside the door behind her. Both men glanced towards it. The German frowned. "I particularly ordered that we should not be interrupted."

The door crashed open. She could not see who stood there. She saw only the absurd amazement on the pink face of the Gestapo man and then, as some automatic weapon sputtered over her shoulder, the spreading gush of blood, like the flowering of some ghastly crimson orchid across his chest.

TWENTY-THREE

For Rick, too, it had been a long day.

Safely back at the caves, physically exhausted but elated by the success of his mission, he snatched a few hours of sleep and then, over breakfast, delighted his friends with a description of the photographs he had obtained.

Once they were developed it would be easier to assess their value. Fortunately Bandini had a good working knowledge of German and as a highly trained army officer he would be well qualified to explain them to the others. But even from Rick's general description it was clear that they would provide a clear picture of the whole military layout in this part of Italy. Not only would Rossi have inside information to help him in planning his guerrilla operations, but much of that information would be worth transmitting by radio to the SOE, to pass on to the Allied commanders. It would fit into the jigsaw that their staffs had to keep constantly up to date.

"A splendid job," said Rossi.

But in that hour of exuberant triumph fell the hammer-blow: an urgent message from Lamberti, brought up by trusted courier. A girl had been caught in the Castle gardens last night and was being held by the Gestapo. It was believed that she was a local girl, his own part-time helper, Lina Scarlatti.

"Damnation!" said Rossi. "We must get her out. At once. At all costs."

Rick, petrified for a moment by the news, stared at him with an awakening hope. Rossi's instant reaction was an immense relief – and somewhat unexpected. He knew the man's hard realistic philosophy. Individuals did not matter, only the eventual triumph of the masses. No room for sentiment. Individuals were expendable – even beautiful girls – the political cause alone was important. But, thank God, he seemed to be treating Lina as an exception.

"But – the Castle!" cried Bernardo. "An army headquarters! How, in God's name —"

"We must find a way. The girl knows too much." Rossi's voice was sombre. There was nothing sentimental, Rick realized, in his approach. "They will break her down. Once she talks, how safe will any of us be? So, we find a way. Before tonight."

Feverishly they discussed all the possibilities. An open attack on the Castle was utterly out of the question. But if a small party of picked men could get in through the Contessa's private entrance...

"If the Contessa will co-operate..." began someone doubtfully.

"Of course she will!" said Rick.

"But —"

"The Contessa is entirely on our side. She showed me those papers. She is a patriotic Italian, she hates the Nazis. And as Comrade Rossi says, if Lina breaks down and talks, none of us will be safe. Least of all the Contessa."

Bernardo was dispatched at once. He would try to find her at the Convent infirmary. There would be nothing suspicious in that – he would explain himself as one of the tenants with an urgent personal problem. The Contessa always showed a kindly concern for everyone on her husband's estate.

A meeting place was fixed at the edge of the forest, as near the town as would be safe from German observation. There Bernardo would report progress to Rossi and the rescue party, who would move down there and stand ready for whatever action proved possible.

There must be one group to get inside the Castle and spirit Lina away. A second group to remain outside and cover their escape. Rossi himself would lead the first group, with Rick and Bandini, whose knowledge of German might be useful. George Wilson and Joe Bateman got themselves included as experienced fighters who had taken part in commando-style operations before.

So much to think of and discuss... possible difficulties, solutions, tactics, this contingency or that... So much to do: weapons to check, sub-machine guns, daggers, tear gas, plastic explosives...

Rick could only be thankful that the urgent hours were filled with the need to concentrate his mind on these practical details. They helped to numb his agonized imagination when he thought of Lina and what she might be going through...

It was early afternoon when Bernardo met them at their rendezvous in the woods. Triumphantly he held up a key. And a sheet of paper, sketching the route from the Contessa's private wing to the part of the Castle that the Germans had taken over for their offices. In the Contessa's familiar florid writing, Rick read her explanatory captions, pin-pointing the room where Lina was most likely to be.

"The Contessa will undertake night duty in the hospital," said Bernardo. "That will be her alibi."

They had already discussed how the rescue party would reach her private entrance without being observed. After last night's events, the Germans might be taking more interest in the gardens.

"She thought of that at once," said Bernardo. "She said it was high time the gardens were cleared and made ready for winter. By now they will be full of workmen, coming and going until dusk. We can mingle with them. Who will notice if we take our chance to slip into one of the grottoes or the shrubberies? Who will count the numbers going home at the end of the day?"

"It will be more comfortable," said Bandini, smiling at Rick, "than lying for hours under the ruins of the Roman villa!"

So the endless day passed, hour after tense hour, bit by bit of the elaborate plan falling gradually into place. Until at last, late in the evening, the Contessa's diagram led their noiseless feet to the right door. Bernardo turned the knob, Rossi went in and his Sten-gun shattered the quiet. Rick was close on his heels, pistol in hand. He saw Collodi – diving for his holster. Bandini fired. The Fascist gasped once and slumped forward over the desk.

Lina sat corded in her chair, her dark head, tousled but unmistakable, sunk on her chest. For a fearful moment Rick thought she might have been hit, being in the line of fire from Rossi's Sten; but she answered instantly to his frantic calling of her name. "Ricardo! Don't touch me – *please*!"

He ignored the instruction, fumbling with the knots.

"This might be quicker," said Joe. The Australian thrust out his big red hand, holding a murderous-looking knife. The severed cord flopped softly to the floor.

Rossi had laid down his Sten. He was gathering up the blood-spattered notes from the desk. Two of his followers had roughly shoved aside the bodies of Collodi and the Gestapo officer and were stripping them of papers, weapons and ammunition. George had somewhere discovered a blanket to wrap round Lina. She was trembling violently. She could not stand without his help.

More guerrillas came in. Their blackened features wore a look of savage satisfaction. "There were only three who had heard anything," one of them reported. He grinned. "They will not hear anything more."

It had happened so swiftly, just as planned. "Give us a little start, Bandini," Rossi said. "We cannot move so fast, because of the girl." Then he saw that George was gathering her up in his arms. The big black man smiled. "I do not think she will be any problem."

"This seems to be your speciality," Rick whispered as they made their stealthy way back along the empty corridors to the Contessa's apartments.

"Guess I'm happier carryin' friends who get hurt than killin' guys I don't know."

With catlike care George descended the spiral stairs, feeling for each tread as he went.

Out in the freshness of the night they hurried across the gardens, alert for any attempt to bar their passage – Rick, Rossi, Joe and the Italians all with their weapons at the ready. The alarm must have been raised inside the Castle even before Bandini's rearguard got clear. They came out shooting. Glancing back across the balustraded terraces, Rick saw the little jets of flame stabbing the darkness. And, as he was clambering through the gap in the boundary wall, a truck full of soldiers came screeching up the avenue from the town.

Rossi had foreseen that. Men detailed for the job had just distributed plastic explosives in the guise of horse-droppings across the road. Now came a brilliant flash, a thunderous echo reverberating from the hills.

"Come!" ordered Rossi.

They raced for the safety of the woods. Bandini's rearguard overtook them after a mile, two of his men slightly wounded, but no one left behind.

"Put me down," begged Lina faintly. But soon she was staggering and the huge American lifted her up again as though she were a child.

"Ricardo?" she whispered.

"I'm still here."

"I told them nothing! You must believe me – nothing!"

"I knew you wouldn't." He groped for her dangling hand and squeezed it.

"As it happens," said Rossi bluntly, "it would not have mattered now. It is an excellent saying, 'Three can keep a secret – if two of them are dead!'"

"Collodi also is dead?" she asked.

Bandini answered from the darkness behind them. "It was necessary – and well deserved. He had collaborated with the Gestapo. He had disgraced the commission he held from the King."

"Where are you taking me?"

"Home," said Rossi. "Where else?"

"Oh, thank *God*!"

Rick also exclaimed. Earlier in the day they had debated whether this would be safe. Now, evidently, the Communist had decided that it would be.

"Both the interrogators are dead," he pointed out. "Any notes they had made are safe in my pocket. And if any Germans come looking for her at the farm they will not find her. The family will see to that. You and our good friend Charlie hid there for weeks in safety. How much easier for her! And there is not an Italian in Sant'Arpino who will say a word."

And so they took Lina safely home.

TWENTY-FOUR

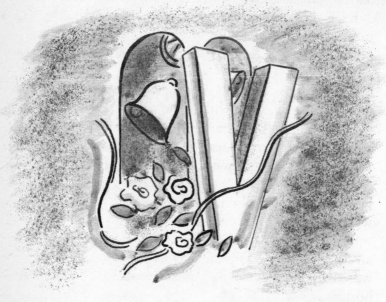

It was a cruel winter that followed, the fighting as bitter as the mountain cold. The armies were deadlocked at the German fortified line. Behind that line the Resistance waged its desperate undercover compaign – hitting and running, harassing the Nazi invaders in every possible way. And, thanks to the inside information in the photographed documents, the Sant'Arpino group was able to demoralize the occupation forces throughout the area.

Then at last, in May, the Allies launched their long-awaited offensive. Americans and British, Canadians and Indians, Free French and Polish hammered the German line until it buckled. To Bandini's delight there was even a reorganized Italian army, the Corpo Italiano di Liberazione, playing its part in the victorious sweep forward up the Adriatic coast.

How long would it be before that advance reached Sant'Arpino?

Each day the tempo quickened. There was a change in the flow of military traffic. No longer were the Nazis pouring troops and supplies southwards. They were pulling out.

"The officers in the Castle are packing up," Bernardo reported after a stealthy visit to the town. "It is said that the Contessa is standing there like a dragon – to see that they do not loot the pictures from the walls!"

The once-sleepy town was becoming a forward base close to the firing line. Convoys of German wounded were passing through. Whole units, battle-shocked, were withdrawing to prepared positions further north.

The sky throbbed with the engines of the Allied aircraft, strengthening their command of the air. Southwards the artillery growled and grumbled beyond the horizon.

Victory was in the air. Fear lifted, one took chances – perhaps foolishly. Lina found an excuse to walk over the mountain top and visit the guerrilla camp, where she had a warm welcome from her former rescuers. To her partly, after all, Rossi owed the information on which he had based so much of his recent success.

"I cannot wait for the Allies to reach Sant'Arpino," she cried.

"Neither can I – *wait*," said Rossi. His tone was so different that she stared at him puzzled. "I must not wait," he went on. "The war will not finish because the bells ring here."

"But —"

"It will not finish while Hitler holds a yard of Italian

soil. A guerrilla's place is always behind the enemy lines. So, when the line moves north beyond Sant' Arpino, we move back ahead of it. We shall fight in the north."

His eyes blazed. He saw, as Rick realized later, what was coming in the months that lay ahead. He saw the partisan forces rising in their tens of thousands to harass the retreating Nazis. He saw the northern cities, Turin and Milan, Genoa and Venice, taken over by the Resistance even before the Allied armies arrived to liberate them. Perhaps even, in his prophetic vision, he saw Mussolini himself meeting his fate at the hands of a guerrilla firing squad.

But all that lay hidden in the future on this May evening in 1944.

Lina turned to the others. "What will *you* do, Joe," she asked the Australian, "when the Allied tanks drive into our town?"

"Ask 'em if they've brought any cold beer! No, seriously, I reckon I'll just go down and report meself."

"Me too," said George. "Nuthin' else we *can* do, or we'll risk bein' charged as deserters. Report for duty. Rejoin our old units – if we can ever find 'em."

"It will be a wonderful day," said Lina. "For you too, Ricardo! And for the poor major, even with his leg – they will be able to bring him out of hiding at last. To see the piazza filled with your comrades – the girls strewing flowers before them and Lamberti opening his best wine —"

The time had come to break the news to her. "I'm afraid," said Rick, "*I* shan't be here."

"Not here? But, Ricardo —" Her eyes were tragic.

"Charlie and I must go with Rossi."

"And at once," said the Communist. "Things are

218

moving fast." Rick drew Lina aside. "I'm sorry – but you must understand. I have my orders."

"Surely you have earned a rest?"

He smiled sadly. War wasn't like that. Rossi worked well with him, they had built up a mutual trust. A new British officer just wouldn't do. Rick must go wherever Rossi went. The group must move north through the mountains, always a little ahead of the retreating Germans, maintaining an unknown menace behind their backs.

Southwards the growling of the guns was a sound of hope and promise, but at this moment it had also a note of sadness and separation. No more jokes together, no more talk of London, no more fantasies of strolling through Soho or taking her to stare through the railings at Buckingham Palace...

"Of course I realize that you must go. I am not a child." But there were tears in her voice. "You will come back, Ricardo? When the war really ends, when it is like the old days in Sant'Arpino – you *will* come back?"

His voice had suddenly gone husky. "What do *you* think?" he said.